FOR MUM

TUESDAYS
ARE JUST
AS BAD

CETHAN LEAHY

MERCIER PRESS

MERCIER PRESS
Cork
www.mercierpress.ie

ISBN: 978 1 78117 564 4

10 9 8 7 6 5 4 3 2

A CIP record for this title is available from the British Library

Printed and bound in the EU.

I

THE STRANGER SONG

ONE

Like many things, it seemed a good idea at the time. Everyone agreed he was ready and should return to a regular routine as soon as possible. 'The longer he avoids it, the worse it will be.' So it was decided: Friday. It was as good a day as any other and, sure, if it didn't go well, it was nearly the weekend. That would soften the blow.

After a gentle prod out of the car ('Honey, try to make the best of it. If things get bad, just call me.' 'Deirdre, stop making it a thing. He's just going to school.' 'See you later.'), he walked through the front gates of the long, red-brick building named after some saint. I followed him. It was my first day too, so I was excited, naturally. I told him as much, but he was not interested. He was going through one of his annoyingly regular bouts of not acknowledging my existence, but I was used to it by now, so it was okay.

The building looked quite grand, though not as glamorous as the American ones on TV. Already I could imagine the shelves inside, resplendent with gold trophies and framed awards, the achievements of their most successful pupils.

Adam hesitated at the white doors. His father said going back would be like ripping off a Band-Aid. Unpleasant, sure, but you can't wear it forever. As he lingered, a mob of second years pushed up behind him, launching him through the door.

Inside was a corridor lined with boys in dreary uniforms with matching expressions. As he walked among them, the talk grew quieter and they stared at Adam, at his visible scar, which was not quite on his forehead, but a little to the side, like a marker that had slipped beyond the line in a colouring book. He walked through them and they couldn't resist looking at it. I thought this was a bit rude.

He didn't stop to speak to anyone in particular, instead walking directly to his locker. But there was no refuge even there. His neighbour, a tall guy with no eyebrows, nodded and nudged him in the side.

'Finally back from holiday, eh, Adam?'

'I am, Billy. Thanks,' said Adam. I was unsure if this was a joke at his expense or just politeness.

'Well, it's good to see you back. I've no one but Mousy to copy off and his notes are crap,' he said, slapping Adam again on the back and walking off.

That wasn't so bad. God bless the Billys of the world.

At this point, I was baffled as to why Adam was so scared to return here. However, it became a bit more obvious when a large lunk appeared behind him, waiting for him to turn around. (I would later learn that this lump was christened Philip M. Hurly.) A broad kid with an untucked shirt and a fussy haircut, he stood staring at Adam with a stupid expression on his face. He coughed dramatically and, once he had Adam's attention, stood still for a moment with a dumb smile, then made a gun gesture with his hand and pointed it at his own temple. 'Boom!' he said and knocked his head back.

A few boys laughed and Adam sank into the floor a foot or two.

'Don't take it so seriously, Adam,' said Philip with a dismissive tone, giving him an insincere ruffle of his hair as he walked away. What a dick.

Anyway, the bell rang and we went to our first class.

***

It was Double Maths and it was *amazingly* boring, like, completely stupefying. Of course, there was no value in the lesson for me, but I found it incredible how anyone could sit through it at all, taking in numbers and lines and letters with no obvious meaning.

So instead of learning about triangles, I floated around the classroom, popping in and out of desks and bags. I spied on the many whispers, text messages and passed notes. There were jokes, questions and some concerns about Adam, to be fair. I told him about them, that they were talking about him. I could tell that he was interested in their reaction, but he pretended instead to focus on some weirdly named shape.

Since I wasn't able to get his attention, I played a little game: 'Who are Adam's friends?' I really hoped that the guy in the corner with the wooden necklace thing was not one, or the blond kid who spent the whole class drawing penises on his neighbour's book. Frankly, they seemed like lost causes. But, as it turned out, he had no friends in that class, or in any class.

***

The bell for morning break rang and Adam slipped away as quietly as he could to hide in one of the bathroom stalls on the far side of the building. Naturally, I followed – who else was I going to talk to? I remained there as he sat in the stall waiting for the second bell to ring.

'Taking a while there, buddy,' I said. No response. Ten minutes later, break ended and the hermit returned to class, having successfully evaded any human interaction. He did this for the full lunch break too, even picking the same stall. Wherever you feel at home, I guess.

***

Back in his non-toilet home, his mother cooked pizza. It didn't look especially appealing but I wouldn't know. I don't eat, so I'm judging it entirely on its looks and it looked like a cat vomited its own tail. She stood, leaning forward, watching him take a bite and she resisted a smile when he finally chewed. He had lost weight since the old hammer swing and so this was a minor triumph.

'How was school?' she said, finally sitting down at the table.

'Fine,' he said without inflection.

'No one said anything, I hope.'

'Nope. Everyone was okay.'

His mother stood up again, filled with nervous energy. 'Where is your father?' she said. 'Usually when I mention food, he's right here.'

As if waiting for his cue, Dad promptly entered the kitchen. He dropped into his seat and immediately picked up his fork. 'Thank you, love! How was school, Adam?'

'Fine.'

'Good to hear.'

'Oh,' said Mum, sitting down again, 'Dr Moore's office called to remind you that your appointment is at 10.30 tomorrow morning.'

Dad glared at Mum with a look that said, 'Deirdre, I'm pretty sure this is not dinner conversation,' to which she responded with a glance that said, 'William, I know but there is no use pretending everything's normal.'

'Okay,' said Adam, who was looking at no one.

To speed this *FASCINATING* dinner along, I can reveal that the night continued in much the same vein. Everyone sat and ate and didn't say anything. After dinner, dishes were washed, dessert was unwrapped and microwaved. We all sat down to watch a movie, *Captain America: The Winter Soldier* – it's about a superhero dressed as a flag. He didn't have very exciting powers, just super strength. I was enjoying it but Adam excused himself about halfway through, saying he was tired. His mother followed him up the stairs to see if he was all right, but Adam assured her he was. I followed too, but I don't have a choice in that.

Without turning on a light, he walked into his room, changed into his pyjamas and lay on the bed. He clearly hoped that this would be the night he would finally fall asleep. He changed his position frequently, shifting his pillows about. However, sleep didn't come. So, instead, he opened his eyes and stared at me, the first time he had looked at me all day.

'Why are you still here?'

I didn't respond. What could I say? I didn't want to be here any more than he did.

TWO

I was born on the same night that Adam died. Born? Is that the right word? I can't say for certain since the logistics of what happened are still unclear to me, but I can say that my first sight was of him lying on the ground with two men leaning over his body. I remember their hands bandaging things and poking others. One said they were losing him, the other agreed and they set about recovering him. They were apparently good at their jobs as they found him again pretty quickly.

I was still here, though, when he came back.

The room was littered with clues to the events that had led up to this moment: a pool of red staining the carpet, a note on the nightstand with some closing remarks and a hammer lying useless on the floor. It was pretty obvious what had happened, even to me who had only existed for three minutes.

Behind me stood a man and a woman. They were well dressed, the man in a fine shirt and the woman in a shiny dress. They stood shaking, not understanding the scene before them (even though, again, it was fairly straightforward). Since they weren't doing anything but staring, I decided that they would be the first people I would communicate with. I waved and the woman burst into tears.

'He's stable,' said one of the men.

They lifted the boy onto a gurney and pushed him into

the ambulance outside. Strangely I was dragged along, as if attached by an invisible rope. So I stood next to him as he faded in and out. The woman in the shiny dress, who had been referred to as the boy's mother, sat next to him and clasped his hand the entire way to the hospital. She was repeating a story over and over; something to do with a cottage and a cow when he was five years old. It sounded like a funny story but her delivery wasn't selling it very well.

They immediately brought him into surgery. I watched as they poked his brain with sharp little knifes and sucked spilt blood with noisy devices (I would later learn these were called scalpels and mini Hoovers). Their hands were acting in unison to recover this mess of a boy in front of them.

The operation was successful. He was brought to a bright room. In the hall, I could hear a conversation between his parents and someone asking a lot of questions.

'Lots of blood lost, but with a stroke of luck there'll be no major brain damage.'

'He has been really down, though. Lots of sleeping,' said his mother. 'I thought he was just … shy.'

'Is there a history of mental illness in the family?'

'Not on my side. His father's great-aunt did once try to walk into the sea on Christmas morning, though.'

'That Aunt Margaret incident is very much up for debate,' his father protested. 'Grandad always maintained she just had too many sherries.'

'Why are you arguing with me about this?'

'It's okay. We are just trying to build up a picture.'

At that point a nurse called from the room, 'He's waking up.'

I watched the boy when he woke in his bright room, surrounded by his parents, doctors and me. I saw his father's tears as he was reunited with his only son. I watched his mother give thanks to someone. They cried and embraced him. But he didn't look at them, instead he looked beyond them, focusing on a spot in the corner of the room, the very spot where I stood.

'Honey, what are you looking at?' asked his mother.

He didn't respond to her question. Instead his eyes widened. He was scared. I moved closer and, with each step, he pushed himself back into his pillows.

'What's wrong?' said Mum.

'He's disorientated,' said a nurse, 'it may be best for you to come back later.'

A second nurse pushed the parents out of the room, reassuring them that 'He'll be fine!'

Soon I was alone with him. I approached the bed and frantically his eyes followed as I got closer and closer.

Finally, he spoke in a whisper. 'Who are you?'

Now I knew for sure he could see me! I was excited, although he did seem a bit more terrified than I'd have liked.

'Don't be frightened,' I said, hearing my own voice for the first time, giving myself a little surprise.

'Are you here to take me away?' he said.

'Where to?'

'I don't know. Hell?'

'Why would I do that?'

'I tried to kill myself.'

'Don't know what that has to do with me.'

He lay back on the bed and closed his eyes. Exhaustion had won and I was alone again.

THREE

I suspected that my presence in Adam's life wasn't appreciated at first. There were subtle clues. He rarely spoke to me. He never discussed my existence with his parents or any doctors. Also, one day, he googled on his phone: 'Can you perform an exorcism on yourself?' As it turns out, the Church was vague on the matter, but he did find a website which featured a surprisingly detailed description of the process, including diagrams and a YouTube video. Unfortunately for Adam, the video mostly advised hiring the services of the host of the video, a sweating American with a dead calm in his voice.

Since Adam did not have the money to hire anyone to throw holy water at him, he went the DIY route. In lieu of holy water, he turned on the shower and, waiting till it got warm, shouted, 'The Power of Christ Compels You!' and jumped in. He seemed disappointed when he got out and discovered that I was still there, instead of being cast out of his presence back to the bowels of the underworld from whence he seemed to think I came. He tried it three more times but I didn't even feel a tingle.

It looked like his best hope for an exorcism was finding a local priest or some manner of holy man skilled at the dispelling of demons and the like. But Adam didn't know any priests as far as I was aware, so I was safe for the moment.

Time moved slowly after the ward. They didn't have the

resources to hold people for long so he returned home with some advice and me in tow. His parents were looking for solutions and there was a lot of talk of going 'private', whatever that meant.

Adam didn't speak to me. He didn't really speak to anyone. He just drifted around the house, keeping his parents on edge. His life was the closest thing to not existing.

'I kinda wish they would leave me alone,' said Adam one day in his bedroom, when there was no one else there. This was the first time he said something when it was just me and him in the room that wasn't 'Go away', 'You don't exist' or 'Bleurgh.' (I'm still not sure what that last one means.)

I wasn't sure if he was talking to me or to himself, but I took the chance. 'They sure are annoying,' I said, rather desperately.

'Yeah,' he said, a little surprised, 'I need a break, you know.'

I nodded. We said nothing more for the day.

***

One morning, he asked me, 'Why are you always hanging around?'

'Can't go anywhere else,' I said. (This was true. Being dragged by the ambulance wasn't a one-off. I couldn't go more than a few metres from him without being blocked by some invisible force. It was a bit of a dose.) 'Besides, I'm pretty sure you are the only one who can see me, so ...'

'I don't talk to you, though. Aren't you lonely?'

'Yeah, I am,' I said, 'but there's not much I can do about it.'

'I'm lonely too.'

'Do you want to talk about it?'

'Not really.'

'Do you want to watch a Netflix?' I said, pointing at his laptop.

He laughed. 'Sure.'

And from that moment we fell into a rather particular routine of watching movies and TV shows for endless periods of time. I was delighted with this. Pretty much everything I learned about this world came from the endless stream of video that poured out of his machine. Granted, it was a little confusing at first (it was a month before I realised that the Avengers were not real people constantly protecting the Earth from aliens or killer robots), but it was invaluable for learning how the world works and what things are called and who the attractive people are.

I was particularly interested in the shows about people Adam's age. They lived such compelling lives. They all went to a big building called a 'high school', had conversations with other people called 'friends'; occasionally two of them smushed their faces together (apparently this is called 'kissing') and often other friends became their enemies because of this face-smushing. I used to ask Adam why his life wasn't filled with sexy adventures like that.

'A: it's the summer. School isn't till September. B: we don't have high school here. It's called secondary school and, alas, no one has sexy adventures,' he said.

'That's a shame, they look fun.'

'They look stressful to me,' he said. 'I couldn't deal with a dance every week.'

'ADAM?' his mother shouted.

'YEAH,' he shouted back, pausing the episode of *iZombie* he was watching. (Zombies, also not real, apparently.)

'Can I come in?'

'Sure.'

The door opened. Evidently, Adam's mother was tired of shouting from beyond. She smiled as usual and I noticed she was carrying some ironed clothes.

'Here's your uniform for tomorrow. How are you feeling about it?'

'About what?'

'Adam, we talked about this. School.'

Adam closed his laptop. 'Tomorrow? School isn't till September.'

'Honey, it is September.'

'I'm not going.' He turned on his bed and faced the wall.

His mother's smile tightened. 'We all agreed it was a good idea. Even you.'

'I'm not ready.'

She sat on his bed. 'You'll probably never feel ready, but you have to go back. You can't avoid school forever.'

SCHOOL! Finally I would see the rich, sexy lives I'd been missing.

'You should definitely go,' I said.

'Don't you miss your friends?' asked Mum.

'What friends?' he said weakly.

Well I was thrilled to finally see the first day of school. Of course, it didn't turn out great in the end, but you already know that.

FOUR

The dog was seated at the table and looked at his owners unhappily. 'I thought we were ordering OUT!' the dog said, apparently able to talk. I didn't get it and I don't think Adam got it either. So he turned the page and looked at the next comic strip, which he also didn't get.

He got irritated, closed the book and returned to playing with his phone. This was a little unfair as I didn't have a phone and was stuck looking at the painting on the wall. It was a landscape of a castle or possibly a cow. Whatever it was, it was not worth the cost of the canvas. I could have painted a better one and I lack the ability to hold a brush.

I looked at the clock. 10.56 a.m. We had already been here ten minutes. Adam's mother had insisted on bringing him in early and had even wanted to wait with him, which Adam was not keen on. This was to be his first session one-to-one with his psychologist, Dr Moore. They had already had some family ones and the next step was separate ones for Adam and for his parents.

Thankfully, the girl at the desk insisted that it was un-necessary for his mother to wait, as she would take good care of Adam. 'Good care' translated into looking up from her computer every so often to make sure he hadn't disappeared.

Finally, Dr Moore's door opened and a young man about Adam's age sauntered out, looking pretty cool. He wore a stylish mishmash of clothes, of a variety which should have clashed but somehow all tied together.

He walked over to the secretary and smiled cheerily, slapping the desk. 'Time for me to go, Dolores, but worry not, for I shall return next week. Same batty time, same batty channel.'

'See you next week, Douglas. Adam, Dr Moore will be ready for you in a few minutes.'

Douglas spun around to look at Adam and grinned. Adam turned his head to ensure that it was in fact him the boy was looking at.

'I see a newbie has taken Alison's spot,' Douglas said. 'I guess this old therapy stuff works, after all.'

Unsure if this was a question, Adam didn't respond. Instead, he looked down at his hands, which intertwined into a nervous nest.

'Ah, the non-chatty type! Well, we are all here for a reason. For example, I have "issues",' said Douglas, making inverted commas with his fingers.

Adam considered this for a moment and, perhaps seeing no value in euphemisms, looked straight at him and said, 'I hit myself in the head with a hammer.'

If this off-the-cuff admission fazed Douglas in any way, he certainly didn't show it. In fact, he laughed. 'That's different. I like it,' he said. 'I do have questions, though, which unfortunately will have to wait. Pressing appointments. See you next week, same batty time, same batty channel!' he said.

Adam didn't know how to respond.

'Hammer, you'll need to be more responsive if we are to get our routine down. We'll never make it to Broadway with this attitude.'

'Oh, eh, yeah,' Adam said, somewhat confused. I think the reference was beyond him; it certainly was beyond me.

'Dr Moore will see you now, Adam,' said Dolores. 'See you next week, Douglas.'

***

'Adam, you should feel free to tell me anything,' said Dr Moore, leaning back in his seat, cool as a cucumber. (I heard someone say that earlier in the week. I have no idea how cool a cucumber is, but from what I understand it is colder than most fruit and vegetables.)

Dr Moore seemed like an okay kind of guy but it was a pretty dull session. In the previous family ones, Adam's mother had filled the room with chatter when any awkward silences had broken out, but now it was just Dr Moore and Monosyllabic Joe.

Adam told Dr Moore next to nothing, just a vague retelling of the information he already had. *Yes, trying to kill yourself is a bad idea. No, he didn't know why he thought a hammer was the way to go. School is fine. Some kids are jerks but what are you going to do?*

I spent most of the time examining the decor of the office. The doctor had a real thing for terrible paintings.

Obviously Dr Moore realised Adam was saying nothing and made an earnest attempt to get him to open up. He wasn't successful. After an hour of no one saying anything of value, the alarm rang. Dr Moore told Adam this was a good start and that they would have the same appointment next week if the time suited. He said there was much to do but that he was looking forward to their journey together. I was confident that he was the only one in the room who felt this way.

***

'That was pointless,' said Adam.

'Not true. At least we got to admire some of his terrible artwork,' I said.

'Oh, yeah, the fire truck painting behind him!'

'Uh, I thought it was a horse.'

We took a shortcut home through the nearby maternity hospital car park, where expectant mothers sat outside, taking a break from being expectant mothers. One watched Adam as he walked by.

By another entrance to the hospital, Adam spotted a group of young people, the loudest of whom was Douglas, the kid from the psychologist's office. With him were two girls and one guy. They were sitting on the wall, talking and laughing. This was the most overt display of camaraderie I had seen during my short existence and I found it fascinating. Adam must have thought so too, since he stopped and stared at them.

One of the girls noticed us – by which I mean 'him' – and said something that quietened down the rest of the group. They all looked over and Douglas stood up.

He waved.

Petrified, Adam gave a tiny wave back and then reached into his pocket for his phone. He pulled it out and pretended to learn something surprising on the screen. This fake message was apparently urgent and, in a pantomime turn, he ploughed forward, his eyes glued to the screen. It was a masterful performance, although a bit unnecessary as they had returned their attention to each other.

In the distance, we could hear them laughing again. Adam blushed and we took the long way home in the hope his embarrassment would have faded by the time he got in the door. When his mother asked how things had gone, he told her the session was fine, everything was fine.

FIVE

Night was a hard time for both of us as he couldn't sleep properly and I simply didn't. I'll admit I quite liked the idea of sleep; everything going into standby for a bit of rest seemed pretty awesome, but it just wasn't a thing that I did. Adam clearly was really into it as he lay in bed each night in hope. But his sleep was always fitful and interrupted at regular intervals. He never got quite there until the weekend following his return to school and his first solo visit to Dr Moore.

Saturday night he slept okay, but on Sunday night he slept like a big baby. I think exhaustion finally won over being kept awake by stress. He didn't turn or stir; it was just a long, nice sleep. I watched him for a bit. Not out of any kind of affection or anything, I was just bored, really, really bored. As I mentioned before, I couldn't leave his presence. I was trapped between these four white-painted walls for the night. Any time I attempted to move out of the room, I slammed against an invisible barrier, like a force field from that *Star Trek* movie we had watched during the summer. (Or was it *Star Wars*? It was a Star Something film anyway.)

Adam looked weird when he was asleep. His arms and legs were spread at bizarre angles, like a masterless puppet. His brown hair seemed to cling to his forehead as if glued there. It was like it knew how important it was to hide his scar at all times, even when in bed.

Once I tired of watching him sleeping, I paced around the room for a while, going through my normal routine of trying to pick things up on his desk, which, as usual, was unsuccessful. I tried this every so often just in case. If it finally worked, then I could find some teenagers and scare them silly. (Adam had been watching a lot of horror movies recently, possibly looking for tips on how to banish me. Fortunately I didn't come in the form of a Victorian doll or a creepy music box, so I was safe.)

I continued circling his bed, really concentrating on how little I had to do. I assume this is why places become haunted – ghosts hanging around with absolutely nothing to do.

After a few minutes of thoughtless movement, I looked up and saw that Adam's bed was in the wrong place. Also it was wider. Also his parents were in it. I'm not going to say how long it took me to realise I wasn't in Adam's room, but in his parents' one next to his, but it was an embarrassingly long period of time. I must have walked through the wall when I wasn't paying attention.

I dashed back into Adam's room. He was still asleep. I jumped back into his parents' room again. This was an important discovery.

It was strange seeing them without Adam. They looked peaceful. Suddenly his dad moved. I made a little jump. He rolled onto his side and wrapped his arm around Mum's shoulders in a faintly protective manner. Perhaps he sensed a spirit in the room. I made an Oooo noise just in case.

I wondered if they ever looked that peaceful when awake.

Perhaps before they realised they had a boy-shaped bomb in the house, one primed to explode. There were various photographs dotted around the house of past adventures and I often looked at them closely for clues. Did they have any inkling about Adam? Were these photos of a happy family taken on the same days that they shared concerned conversations in bed about how Adam doesn't talk as much as he used to, or how he didn't seem to have friends? Perhaps these were days when everyone was happy and there was no reason to question it, as if happiness was a vampire that if exposed to light would shrivel. These were possibly interesting questions I'd have dwelled on if I wasn't suddenly able to get out of the gaff.

Passing their bed, I approached their closed door and slipped through it to find myself on the landing.

I walked down the stairs.

I walked out the front door.

I was outside.

The street lamps peeked between the tree branches and they buzzed as I moved underneath. I didn't question my new freedom. I just kept going. The row of houses swished by as I sped ahead of their next-door neighbour, who was out running at this odd time. There was music somewhere. I followed it.

I followed it along the river that slunk through the city.

I followed it over the bridge.

I followed it to the centre of town, where drunks and loud music abounded, and men and women bumped into each other and laughed. They dared each other at the bridge and kissed each other sitting on window sills. I passed through them, hoping to experience their electricity. There were two men having a fight against a fountain as people cheered. There was a loud queue for food in cardboard boxes. This world was unfamiliar to me. They were happy and angry and sad and everything. I was so used to 'numb', I never imagined what other real-life emotions would look like. Facing so many new ones all at once was suddenly overwhelming, so I decided to find somewhere calmer.

I went further. To the suburbs, where nothing happens and there is always a dog barking in the distance. Adam lived close to the city, so there was always at least a hum of activity, but it was so quiet here, kind of like how I imagined sleeping to be. There was no one to be seen, except one person standing outside his front door staring at the night sky.

That person was a boy, much like other boys. He wore the same uniform as Adam, but didn't look at all like him. This guy was more handsome and somehow looked more at home in his uniform. Most of the guys in school looked as if their uniforms didn't fit, but not this kid. He also had a content expression which I had never seen before.

I was confused, though. What time was it? It had to be past midnight. He must really like school if he was still wearing his uniform in the middle of the night. I wished I could ask what he was doing.

As if reading my thoughts, he looked at me and smiled.

'See you later,' he said and just disappeared, smile and all.

SIX

Probably since it was unused to sleep, Adam's body got greedy and took more than it needed that night, so, as a result, the next morning he was late. Launching himself out of bed, he ran down the stairs with his school tie half strangling him. He dashed into the kitchen where his mother was listening to the radio.

'Mum, I'm late! Why didn't you wake me?' he said, grabbing a banana from the fruit bowl.

'Oh, I thought you needed the rest. I'm sure the school will understand.'

Adam sighed, as Mum unravelled and fixed his tie. 'Everyone always understands. I just don't want to be late. Can I have a lift?'

The closer we got to the school, the more his mood improved. But he didn't share my enthusiasm for the previous night's discovery.

'I thought you weren't able to leave,' Adam whispered as we rushed through the gates.

'Oh, it looks like I can when you're asleep. I tried this morning when you woke up and no dice!'

He shook his head. 'There is no way someone saw you.'

'He was right in front of me. He was tall, had blond hair. His ears were kind of sticky out. He was wearing your school uniform, though. You may be able to find him here,' I said.

'I thought he disappeared.'

'I think he did. Maybe he stepped back into the house. I don't know how this all works.'

'Well, neither do I. Wait! Stop! People can't see me talking to thin air. Everyone thinks I'm weird enough as it is.'

'Okay, but do you know who I'm talking about?'

'No. He's not real, because you're not real. I know you're a hallucination. Just leave me alone.'

'Hallucination? Could a hallucination do this?' I said, before I floated up above his head and down the other side.

'Yes. Doing impossible things is the definition of a hallucination,' he said at full volume and then gasped like a cartoon character when he realised what he'd said was loud enough for the rest of the school to hear. Fortunately for him, there was no one around. He checked his mobile for the time.

'Crap. I definitely missed the bell,' he said.

We entered the front door and walked down one of St Jude's many corridors. The school seemed to be ninety-five per cent corridors of large blocks painted white, resembling something made from a dull set of toy bricks. (*Coming Soon: The Educational Establishment Kit. Literally Seconds of Fun.*) And they were very long too. If you were alone in them, they seemed infinite.

When we made it to the door of his classroom, he took a moment to prepare an apology. He didn't get to use it, though, since the room was completely empty. He walked out and checked the next classroom, it was empty too. Not a sole student to be seen.

'Wait, is it the right day?' he said. 'How long did I sleep?'

From the hall came the echo of talking. In a moment the voices turned the corner into our corridor and it was clear that it was two second years.

'What is this for anyway?' said the shorter of the two.

'I heard somebody died. Hey, d'you reckon that guy finally did … Ow!' said the taller one, his yelp caused by a hard dig in the arm. He started to protest but then saw Adam standing in front of him and realised his mistake. The younger boys both smiled awkwardly and walked past Adam. Once they thought they were out of earshot, they started to laugh about what a noob the taller one was.

Adam followed them to the school theatre room, or 'the auditorium' as Principal O'Neill insisted on calling it. It was primarily used for visits from the lord mayor, cheerleading for upcoming rugby matches and, as it turned out, delivering bad news about fellow students. It was filled with the whole school. There was the usual noise that comes from packing lads of varying ages in a room, so Adam was able to sneak in largely undetected. The few who did look behind them to see who had come in appeared stunned, as if a zombie had walked in.

A teacher, Mr Banks, spotted Adam and pointed to an empty seat on the aisle next to Redmond. I think I mentioned Redmond before. He was the nervous kid who doodled impulsively on people's books in class. I once watched him draw a record amount of Spidermen with large penises in the margins of an unsuspecting *Exploring Physics 3* book.

Redmond made a little noise when Adam sat down next to him. 'Adam! Oh, I thought that you were ... I ... never mind. Sorry, ignore me,' Redmond said, so Adam did.

Mr O'Neill, the principal, appeared. He was a tall, skinny man with clouds of grey hair on his head. He stood in the centre of the stage area and coughed loudly. 'Settle down,' he began. 'I regret to have to inform you all that a tragedy has occurred.'

He continued on, his speech pretty dull, and, to be honest, it isn't really worth my while repeating the entire thing. It just kind of went on and on, although it had a few meaningful sentences scattered through it. The key piece of information – and this is important – is that there had been a death in the school, a fellow student.

That student was Chris Hurly: star rugby player, excellent student and, from what I gathered, a popular fellow. There was a noticeable gasp when his name was revealed. I couldn't recall him being mentioned before now, but then I hadn't been here too long and all the names and faces kind of blurred into one. (Adam later explained to me he was a sixth year, people liked him, and also that he was the older brother of Philip, the dick from the first day, who for obvious reasons wasn't in attendance that day.)

As far as I could tell, the main reason for the meaningless-ness of the principal's speech was that he was dancing around how Chris died. He was being very vague about the cause of his demise, giving few details, if any. But Adam and I had our suspicions; most likely it was the one fate of young men that no one likes to speak of. When we all filed out of the assembly room, there was immediate talk and it was clear the masses were not as perceptive.

'I heard he was in a gang and he got murdered.'

'Nah baiy, a neighbour said he was having a wank with a belt around his neck and tightened it too much.'

No one asked for Adam's guess, but he didn't have time to answer as a female teacher tapped him on the shoulder.

'Could I speak with you for a moment, Adam?' she said.

'Well I have Bossy for CSPE now; I mean Mr Busey.'

She smiled. 'Don't worry. I'll have you back to Bossy in a few minutes.'

They walked into her office, a small room above the gym. On the door was sellotaped a makeshift sign, a sheet of A4 protected by a transparent sleeve, the kind you put into folders. It said 'Miss Costigan, Guidance Counsellor' in large writing.

'Sit down, Adam,' she said, pulling out a seat for him at her desk and picking up some leaflets resting on it. 'You'll have to excuse the mess. I've just moved in.'

'Yes, Miss Costigan.'

'None of that – call me Sandra. Or Sandy if you like beaches.'

This joke got no reaction, so she chuckled herself lest a vacuum occur.

'Anyway, Adam, I brought you in here to tell you that … there is nothing confirmed but it is looking very likely that Chris killed himself.'

Adam said nothing, but he did blink.

'Ah … It's probably best I don't go into details. But we felt that given your recent difficulties it was best to warn you in advance that you will be getting a lot of reminders or "triggers" if you will. I discussed it with your teachers and we are willing to give you the rest of the week off if you think you need it.'

'No thank you, Miss. I just want to get back to normal,' said Adam.

Miss Costigan smiled a sad smile that said she sympathised and God love 'im. 'I admire your bravery. Okay, you can return to class. Oh, and also, I would appreciate it if you didn't tell anyone about Chris. I'm sure they will find out soon enough but it would be good to not have the school awash with scandal for a day at least.'

Adam nodded and walked out the door. Down the corridor, a first year ran past, bashing into him. 'Sorry! Hey, did you hear? Someone topped himself!'

***

Adam spent that night looking at Chris's Facebook page. It hadn't yet been turned into an official memorial page, but the timeline was filling up with tagged photos of happier times and captions like RIP MY FRIEND and TOO GOOD FOR THIS WORLD.

Sad Face.

Adam scrolled down through each one and read the comments underneath, long paragraphs on the cruelty of life with thirty-two likes and growing.

'Is that him?' I asked.

He nodded and I, perhaps not in keeping with the solemnity of the moment, got excited. 'That's the guy I saw. The disappearing boy,' I said.

'What is wrong with you? The guy is dead,' Adam said, closing his laptop.

I was about to explain why this was exciting when there was a knock on the bedroom door, his father's signature rat-a-tat of three.

'Adam?' he called.

'Yeah? I'm on the phone,' he said, pulling out his phone to make his story believable. Which might have worked except his parents knew he had no friends.

'Can I come in?'

Adam didn't respond to this, which Dad took as a non-objection and slowly walked in. Miss Costigan had rung earlier to tell his parents what had happened so that they would be prepared. His mother had attempted to talk about it when Adam got home, with little result. The subject was further avoided at dinner, when his father gave it a shot and was ignored.

'Are you okay?' Dad said.

'I didn't know him.'

His father smiled faintly. There had been a lot of smiles with mysterious meanings aimed at Adam that day.

'It's still okay to feel sad if someone you don't know dies.'

Adam shrugged.

'Ah, Adam, I don't want to put too much pressure on you, but when stuff like this happens in school, you can talk to me or your mother about it.'

'I know, Dad.'

They watched each other for an awkward minute. In the end, Dad patted Adam's shoulder. 'We're watching a movie downstairs if you want to join.'

'No thanks, I'm tired. I think I'll just have an early night.'

I'd seen this conversation a million times. In fact, it felt like the only conversation I'd seen. I was hostage to this conversation. When his dad left the room, Adam reopened his computer, his sad, morose face scanning more posts. I looked at the deceased in photos of more pleasant times and I felt that apparently inappropriate excitement bubble up again. He looked exactly like the boy I'd seen.

II
EVERYBODY KNOWS

SEVEN

It was my first funeral, so I was determined to enjoy it. It was a week after the incident and the relevant people were satisfied that there was no foul play and that Chris's death was indeed a case of self-destruction. This meant it was time to put him in the ground.

The funeral took place in a small church somewhere in the greener part of the city. Everyone from his year and Philip's year was there. I believe the idea was to form a united front, an army of mourners, or warriors of grief if you are feeling romantic. They didn't look very convincing, though. The assembled students looked uncomfortable, unsure how to act in this unfamiliar place.

Adam was especially twitchy that day. He was given permission beforehand to not attend, given his 'condition'; in fact, Dr Moore had emphasised that he thought it was a bad idea for him to go. But Adam waived the permission, saying that he didn't want to make an issue of it (although I personally felt he was making it more of an issue by going). The vice-principal told him that he admired his desire to get on with things. I, however, was baffled that he turned down yet another opportunity to skip school.

Outside the church, various adults spoke in hushed but surprisingly cheerful voices. I thought they would be discussing their memories of Chris, but instead they appeared to be taking advantage of the boy's death to catch up on what had happened since the last funeral within their circle.

The church was a modest building, certainly not on the scale of the massive cathedrals I had seen in vampire films. In fact it looked surprisingly cosy among the trees and in the unseasonal brightness of the day. Good burying weather, I guess.

Led by Brother Dermot, the RE teacher, the students were squeezed into several rows of seats in the back and were told to wait in silence for the service to begin. Not knowing what to do, they sat there watching the grieving family as the priest prepared at the altar. Philip was positioned at the edge of the front pew, looking everywhere but at the gleaming coffin in the centre of the aisle.

Suddenly the organ erupted with a song that I didn't know the name of, but which didn't seem to be a church hymn. I'm guessing it was one of Chris's favourites. (I noticed a boy from Adam's year take his phone out to record it.)

The organ came to a hush when the priest took to the altar and everyone stood up. The mass had begun.

Throughout the ceremony, Adam was transfixed, watching the deceased's family carefully as they struggled to retain a presentable face. If I had to guess, the main thought going through his mind was that this served as an alternative-universe peek at what his funeral would have been like. Instead it would be his father grimly staring at the coffin, his mother crying so hard that it distorted her face into a horrifying mask.

The priest gave a sincere, Wikipedia-style synopsis of the deceased's life. This was occasionally interrupted by various family members who walked up to the lectern and said their pieces and prayers, some struggling to finish their simple offering. When his turn came, Philip gave a little speech on his now deceased sibling. It had some mild jokes in it but what really struck me was Chris's impressive list of accomplishments, although I think it was a mistake to list them all, as it emphasised what a tragic loss his death was. It would probably be easier to mourn people if it appeared that they contributed less to our lives.

The mass came to an end. The coffin was lifted by men in black suits and they passed us by, bearing the weight with surprising ease. Taking advantage of my ghostliness, I took a little peek inside but it was too dark to see anything. Nighttime in a box. It was carried out to a really long, black car waiting outside.

Once loaded, people approached the family to pay their respects. There was a lot of shaking of hands and people saying sorry. Not sure why – they didn't kill him. Unsure what to do, Adam stepped towards Philip, but was squeezed out by the other students. This was no loss, however, since Philip seemed distracted.

I wanted to follow them to the burial but it was only for close friends and family, so Brother Dermot escorted the rest of the students back to school. The bus was in no great rush and Adam stared out the window, watching the buildings pass by. No one sat next to him, probably thinking he'd rather be left alone with his own thoughts. Although, even in normal times they felt no requirement to speak to him, so Adam sitting on his own was actually not uncommon.

On the way, we passed a graveyard. I wondered if it was the same one that Chris was headed to. It looked nice.

'Hey, I just realised something,' I said to Adam, having just realised something.

'What?' he said quietly.

'I'm a ghost who has never been to a graveyard.'

Adam snorted. Unfortunately, he did this on a bus filled with mourning students, but they already thought he was weird, so it didn't lower his reputation any further.

EIGHT

In that week's session, Dr Moore was playing with a pen in his hand as he asked, 'What made you decide to go to the funeral? I did strongly recommend that you shouldn't attend.'

This was our third solo visit to the psychologist and Adam was slowly becoming more open. In fact, the whole situation was quickly turning into a routine: Adam turned up with his mother; that Douglas kid would come out of his appointment and say hello in some bizarre way; followed by an hour of Dr Moore asking questions, nothing but questions. Perhaps he only spoke in questions.

'Did you feel somehow *obliged*?' Dr Moore said.

'I guess,' Adam said.

'How did the funeral make you feel?'

Adam leaned back and looked up at the ceiling for the moment. 'Strange. I didn't really know him other than that his brother is in my class. Like, he is … was very popular, and a star on the rugby team, which is very important in our school. They are like gods. I think he even won some awards for, um, rugbying.'

'Do you think that was important?'

'Not to him apparently.'

'Adam.'

'Obviously I felt sad for his family, but I dunno, he had so much potential, it almost makes it seem more tragic than if …'

Adam let the sentence trail off, its meaning pretty clear.

'Adam, I must emphasise to you that there is no ranking to suicides: each is as tragic as the others. Don't fall into the trap of thinking that somehow you would be missed less because you don't have a shelf full of sports trophies,' said Dr Moore.

'I guess. It's just, if a top rugby player with lots of friends could commit suicide, anyone could.'

NINE

A tanned couple on a beach.

A smiling man on skis.

Another couple drinking wine outside a café.

A vast array of images of humans having good times flicked by on Mum's laptop. She was on a website called Holidaze.ie. Adam had once again gone to bed early, thus freeing me up to observe his parents in their natural habitat – the TV room. Mum sat across the couch with her feet on the armrest and Dad sat in an armchair, flicking through the many channels they had in the faint hope of finding something interesting enough to hold his attention for at least a few minutes. They looked more relaxed than usual.

'I was thinking we should go somewhere. It would be something to look forward to,' Mum said, to which Dad replied, 'We probably should check with Dr Moore first, but that sounds like a good idea.'

He switched the channel and settled on the news.

'Can you change the channel? I'm sick of news for today.'

'Sorry,' Dad said, before embarking on a merry jaunt through the movie channels. It may surprise you to learn that Mum's job wasn't solely walking into Adam's room and looking slightly mournful while smiling when talking to him. During the day she read the news bulletins on the local community radio station. It explained the times where she appeared to be unusually well-informed on what roadworks were happening where and which TD said something they shouldn't have.

'Oh, what I would give to live in a bubble for a day and hear nothing of the world,' she said, closing the laptop. Sensing it was time for a conversation, Dad lowered the volume on the TV, having settled on an episode of *Inspector Morse* (a show about a guy who solves murders by listening to lots of opera).

'Bad news day so?' he said.

'It's nothing but constant misery. I tell you, I feel like Atlas carrying the weight of the world on my back,' she said, confusingly comparing herself to a book of maps.

'At least you are still getting to use your Classical Studies degree for jokes,' Dad said.

'Did you hear another boy killed himself? Somewhere up past the station,' she said.

'I hadn't heard.'

'Poor kid. In work we were given these guidelines for reporting suicides. You know, don't glamorise it, don't detail the method. I wish life was like that. Someone out there editing our lives, keeping out the rotten details.'

'The poor parents,' said Dad.

'I sometimes fear that one day I'll have to report Adam's death.'

'I think they would give you the day off.'

'Har har.'

'How do you think he is?' Dad said, suddenly serious. 'I like to think he is doing better.'

'He does seem more – not cheerful – but less gloomy since he went back to school,' she said. 'The sessions with Dr Moore seem to have helped.'

'It's been three months since it happened and I still have no idea why he did what he did.'

'Remember what Dr Moore said. It's not anyone's fault. Adam is a depressed kid and depression is sneaky.'

'That's not very helpful,' Dad groaned. 'I mean, he doesn't have a terrible life. He goes to a good school, has loving parents, regular food. He's quite lucky, really.'

'I think he knows that. The trouble is, I guess, that the D word turns everything into ash. He just has to work harder than everyone else to be happy.'

'Hardly seems fair.'

'I'd feel better if he had some friends. He's shut us out. I imagine he must be so lonely. You know, I think I've heard him talking to himself on occasion. I'm going to mention it to Dr Moore next time.'

'At least we're more prepared, aren't we?' his dad said. 'If there is a next time, we'll see it coming.'

'I hope so.' Mum sighed and opened the laptop again. The mood lightened once more as she clicked on a picture of a grinning woman by a pool.

'Enough of old Miss Misery. How was your work today?'

'Oh, same old, same old. We tried to start the new project, but Harry was late for the meeting.'

I had learned that Adam's dad was in IT but what his

actual job entailed was very unclear. The only things I knew for certain were that it involved computers and Harry was useless and it was only a matter of time until he was fired. As Dad proceeded to drone on about work, I took the opportunity to wander out into the night.

TEN

In Adam's room the blue carpet is a little too wide, so it curls up when it meets the skirting board on the left side of the room. There is a desk on which there is typically a tower of school books, a framed photograph of a deceased grandfather and a loose pile of papers, pens and other stationery. There are two posters on his wall. One is for the movie *Sin City* and features an attractive woman with a lasso. The other is a poster of a band, The XX, and the integrity of the Blu Tack holding it up on the top right-hand corner was beginning to falter.

There is a single bed with a plain set of sheets and duvet cover, though when these are in the wash there is a second set covered with multiple versions of a weird-looking creature apparently called a Pikachu. There is a bookshelf with the following books standing in this exact order from left to right: *The Outsiders* by S. E. Hinton (unread), *The Hunger Games* by Suzanne Collins (unread), *To Kill a Mockingbird* by Harper Lee (read), *The Stand* by Stephen King (half read), *The Hitchhiker's Guide to the Galaxy* by Douglas Adams (quarter read), *The Enemy* by Charlie Higson (read), *The Catcher in the Rye* by J. D. Salinger (three-quarters read). There is a window made up of four panels which has a handle that can be twisted in such a way that you can slightly open it or open it fully. On the ceiling there is a yellow stain, most likely from a leaking pipe, which, if you look at it from a certain angle, resembles half a bicycle.

Is this getting tedious? Try living there. I spend so much time in this room with Adam's cheerless company that I can recount in specific detail every inch of the stupid place. For the best part of a month we went nowhere but this room, Dr Moore's office, Adam's school and the routes between the three. If it wasn't for my night-time rambles and the odd funeral, I'd have gone mad. Still, I wanted to see more of the world when everyone wasn't asleep.

So one Saturday afternoon I requested that we go for a walk.

'You can,' he said, all his attention on a movie he was watching on his laptop. I was beginning to grow tired of that thing. The recent picks were all pretty terrible too, except one with a creepy-looking rabbit man. I enjoyed that one, although I couldn't tell you what it was called.

'No, I can't,' I insisted. This was true. After some experimentation, I had worked out that I could only go out on my own when he was asleep, and it had to be a pretty deep sleep at that. I still hadn't figured out the reason for this. My working theory was since ghosts usually haunt a specific house, perhaps I haunted a specific depressed teen.

'Well, sucks to be you so,' he said, shrugging. He may have thought that he had the upper hand but this time I had a plan, a finely tuned scheme to convince him that leaving this hole of a room would be mutually beneficial. This cunning idea I devised upon careful observation and ingenuity. I had noticed that when he passed the radio in the kitchen that his mother left on when she was doing whatever mothers do, he would turn down the volume to the lowest setting when a certain ad jingle was playing, a song that goes a little something like this:

'When you can't get a sandwich out of your head …'

'What?' he said with surprise, distracted from the zombies destroying New York. Since I had never tried it before, my singing could most generously be described as enthusiastic. Also I'm not sure I'd got the lyrics right.

'Buy yourself a pan of Healy's Bread.'

'Stop!' he said, trying to block his ears with his hands. 'I hate that ad.'

I turned up the volume. 'When you want toast with some spread …'

'How can something with no physical throat sing so badly?' he said, lifting a pillow and wrapping it round his head.

I leaned in close. 'Buy yourself a pan of Healy's Bread.'

'Why do you hate me?' he said, throwing the pillow at me. Not surprisingly, it passed straight though me, and then knocked into The XX's poster behind me, causing it to finally lose its grip on the wall. I continued to sing, as I could see I was really getting to him. On my fourth rendition of 'WHEN YOU CAN'T GET A SANDWICH OUT OF YOUR HEAD', he cracked.

'FINE! We'll go for a walk, if you'll just stop!'

'Oh yay,' I said. I was victorious; also I wanted a sandwich, despite my lack of stomach.

***

In the daylight, town was a strange and marvellous place, certainly in comparison to Adam's private cell or the inside of the school building. For one, it was full to the brim with things. As we walked, we passed parks, shops, churches and dogs, bright dresses, pure white tracksuits, large jumpers and long jackets, scarves of all stripes, jeans with weird holes torn into the side revealing goosepimply skin.

I suggested to Adam that he should start dressing in a more interesting way. He seemed unreceptive, but I was not surprised. He mostly appeared to dress out of necessity: T-shirts, jeans and nondescript jumpers.

We reached our destination, the large Boots at the end of Paul Street. When he had told his mother that he was heading to town, she asked him to pick up her special shampoo. We couldn't remember what it was called, but we knew it came in a blue bottle and we were pretty sure the name rhymed with 'sports cough'.

This was completely different. Inside were rows of toothpastes and deodorants, women with their hair up in elaborate towers, who stood in front of their booths waiting for their next customer on whom to practise their arts of illusion. They could make you look younger. They could make you smell fresher. They could remake you into something more attractive. With a little bit of effort, you could look a lot more appealing – I'm not sure to whom, but it was clear there was a kind of magic here.

We passed them swiftly enough and stood in the shampoo section. There were many, many different types of shampoo.

'Is it that one?' Adam said, pointing at a blue one.

'I have no idea.'

'Can I help you?' said a woman in a clean white smock, stacking conditioners.

'Oh, ah, um … I'm looking for a shampoo that is blue and sounds like "sports cough",' said Adam.

The woman immediately handed him the correct one.

'Oh, it's German. Thank you.'

Adam dutifully bought the bottle of shampoo. Having accomplished his one task in town, he decided to walk in the vague direction of home, which is how we ended up in a brick-paved area next to a shopping centre where I was amazed to see happy teenagers. And not just a few – there were loads. They stood under the tree that seemingly grew through the pavement in the centre. They sat against walls and under the sole tree with half-drunk bottles of Club Orange or Coke, using their mobile phones to play music. They drank tea on rickety seats outside cafés. They wore weird clothes, and hats covered hair of unnatural shapes and colours. They had piercings and sunglasses (even though it was closer to winter than summer) and laughter and everything. As you can imagine for the all-boys private-school-goer, the most alarming aspect was that there were teenage girls, many of them in fact.

Whatever this place was, it was a brave new world for us to explore and naturally, since he was a big baby, Adam decided he wasn't doing this any more.

'I … I have to go home. Mum will be worried if I'm too long,' he said checking his phone, which had no messages.

'Relax,' I said, 'she was clearly cool with this.'

This was probably not true. Though she was glad he had left his room, she did fear not being in the immediate proximity of him in case of you never know what, so she had made him promise he would text her in the event that something happened or, indeed, if nothing happened.

'I don't think so,' said Adam. 'We should get back.'

'Oh come on!' I said. 'Foot stamp noise!' (I couldn't stamp my foot.)

'Hey, Hammer!' said a voice.

The owner of the voice was Douglas, the batty channel guy from the psychologist's office. He was holding court over a pot of tea in front of one of the cafés with the group of kids from the maternity hospital.

'Ah … I'm not mad about that nam–'

'Wanna join us? It looks less weird if you are in a crowd when you are talking to yourself.'

I certainly wasn't going to let Adam pass up the chance to expand his horizons.

'We should join them,' I whispered in his ear.

Unsure, but too polite to run away screaming, Adam walked towards the table. 'Sure, ah, my name isn't Hammer. It's Adam.'

'Hi, Adam!' they all said in unison.

Douglas kicked a chair across from him from underneath

the table. It didn't shift as intended but the sentiment was obvious. The girl next to the empty seat pulled the chair out the rest of the way for him. Douglas stood up and spread his hands out in a flourish, inviting Adam into his domain.

'Well, Adam Hammer, let me introduce you to the whole gang. This tall girl, who was so kind as to pull out your seat and comes covered with positively shocking yellow hair and a carefully curated collection of badges on her jacket, is Linda.'

'Charmed,' said Linda.

'Hi,' said Adam, offering his hand. She shook it with a false daintiness which clearly embarrassed him. I wondered what her hand felt like.

'This young man in the striped jumper that has "Dead Flowers" emblazoned on the front is Barry, and no, we don't know what that is supposed to mean. He is short and very chatty,' Douglas continued, pointing at the solemn-looking young man.

'Hi,' said Adam.

A grunt was his response.

'And this Gothy lady, who is rudely writing something down as I speak—'

'Sorry.'

'… is Aoife.'

'Hi,' she said, looking up from a notebook with a design of two skeletons in an embrace on the cover. Her clothes had a lot of studs in them.

'Hello,' Adam said with a nod.

'And you know me from our little tête-à-têtes every Saturday morning, but in the very unlikely event you don't recognise me in a different environment, I'm Douglas, the Lord of Paul Street.'

'Hah,' said Aoife.

'Quiet you! Combined, we are the … group of people who have yet to settle on a name for their group.'

'How do you two know each other?' asked Aoife.

'I–' said Adam, before he was interrupted.

'We share a psychologist. Remember, you saw him a few weeks ago when we were hanging out at the hospital. Adam here tried to kill himself with a hammer.'

Dick move, Douglas. Not only did this bald statement silence everyone and leave Adam to flounder, it also ruined the possibility of hinting at a cool secret past, like on TV. One that could include Paris and a torrid affair with a governor's wife, and didn't involve ineffective suicide methods. All ruined now.

'I was never any good at DIY,' said Adam.

What was this strange sound? Laughter? Adam had said something vaguely witty and people enjoyed hearing him say it. This really was a day of miracles. Feeling welcome, Adam sat down, but the moment his bottom touched the seat …

Beep beep!

Adam checked his phone.

Hey, I'm passing through town from Ciara's, if you are feeling lazy and want a lift home. xx

'Girlfriend?' said Linda. 'Sorry, we hold no manner of secrets in the group that has yet to find a name.'

'No, it's my mum.'

'Well, don't be a cad of a son, text her back immediately,' said Linda. I made a note that she deeply respected the bond between son and mother. It seemed important to remember things about people if you wished to become their friend.

> It's okay Mum. I met some friends. Will be
> home in an hour.

> No rush! See you for dinner.
> Xxxx

The extra 'x's suggested that Adam's mother was completely on board with this friendship making.

'So before I rudely made you join us, we were discussing … what were we discussing?' said Douglas.

'I don't think we were discussing anything,' said Linda.

'We have been sitting here for an hour. We had to be talking about something.'

'The best ways to eat a banana?' suggested Barry.

'No, that was yesterday,' said Aoife, 'on Facebook.'

Linda made an expression of pure fury and slammed her paper cup on the table. 'I was not invited to this banana discussion, despite being a known enjoyer of bananas!'

'I don't want to talk about bananas,' said Douglas.

'You are not the ruler of this conversation, Douglas,' said Linda.

'One day, Linda, one day.'

'Wait, is there more than one way to eat a banana?' asked Adam.

Douglas shook his head. 'Oh, Adam, you have much to learn.'

They literally spent the next hour talking about bananas, tackling such subjects as how many bananas you can eat before dying of potassium poisoning, if the fact that the ridges perfectly match the shape of your hand is proof of God's existence and the curious statistic that Ireland was the largest exporter of bananas in the world. (The last point was Adam's contribution. Apparently bananas from around the world are imported into Ireland and then sent out again all over the world. I'm unclear how he knew this as he had never spoken of an interest in bananas before.) While I was a little confused by the pointless nature of this discussion, it was a strange relief to not have the cloud of Adam's condition hanging over it.

Eventually, due to impending dinners, the group scattered to catch their respective lifts and buses, but not before they all gave Adam their numbers, except Douglas, who firmly did not believe in mobile phones and was only contactable through the landline, post and Facebook.

'See you later,' Adam said.

'GOODBYE, NEW FRIEND!' they shouted as they split up.

ELEVEN

Sunday morning came and it was approaching that time for Adam's parents' weekly enquiry if he wanted to go for a family walk. They were obsessed with walks. I wondered aloud if this was a sign that they really wanted a dog rather than a son. Adam rolled his eyes at this suggestion and instead informed me that they had read somewhere that walks were a good idea for someone suffering from depression. I countered that while this may be true, it was still entirely possible that they would prefer a dog. He did not appreciate this.

A knock on the door, bang on schedule.

'Hey, your father and I are thinking of heading towards Garretstown for an old stroll if you fancy,' said Mum, popping her head in. She was good at popping her head in. Adam looked out the window at the grey day outside.

'All right.'

His mother smiled.

'Cool,' she said.

In the car there was a big discussion about which radio station to listen to.

'You know,' said Dad, 'I knew I had gotten old when I didn't understand what the music on the radio was. Is that a robot singing?'

'Who is this? Adam, do you like this?' added his mother.

'It's okay, I guess,' said Adam.

'I was mad about music when I was your age. I was a Blur kid. I was even the drummer in a tribute band, "Parklite". Although I only had a drum machine, not a proper drum kit.'

When this got no reaction, he continued. 'However, horrors of horrors, your mother was into Oasis, but I learned to live with that.'

'What does that mean?' I asked and Adam shrugged.

'Very funny. What do you listen to, Adam? What are the young people into today?' asked his mum.

'I dunno. I don't really listen to music.'

'Oh, "Common People"! Leave this on. I love this one. You know this, right?'

After fifteen minutes of listening to whatever the hell the nineties was, we arrived at the beach. It didn't seem to have many people on it as it was Ireland and nearly winter. I am an intangible being of unclear origin and even I knew it was too cold for a swim.

'It's good to be out and about,' said Dad to no one in particular as they climbed over some rocks.

I had never been to the beach before. The sea was impressive; it really did not look like it ended anywhere.

'The water is bleak enough,' said Dad.

They jumped down and landed safely on the sand. On a closer look, Adam's father was right. The sea did look bleak. As they trudged along the edge of the water, Adam said nothing, instead watching a boat floating far away on the horizon. It looked like a toy from here.

'It's been a long while since we were last here,' said Mum.

'It's only a few months,' said Adam.

'June, wasn't it?' said Dad. 'Remember, we ran into Jason's brother?'

'Oh, is that all? Seems longer.'

'It is late September. That was a while ago.'

They walked more in silence, perhaps remembering that sunny day they met Jason's brother, whoever that was. The wet sand made a sombre plop with each step. I could hear a panting noise and saw a large, fluffy creature rapidly approaching. The closer it got, the clearer it was that it was one of those big hairy dogs from the paint ads on TV. Leash flapping in the wind, it had clearly escaped from its owner. It skipped past Adam and rubbed up against Dad.

'Oh, hello boy!' said Dad, petting him.

'He has a lovely coat, doesn't he, Adam?' said Mum.

Adam grunted.

'Sorry about that. He just wants to play,' said an out-of-breath woman who had just arrived.

'No worries.'

'Come on, Hobbes,' she said, taking his leash and walking away. When she was gone, Mum started talking with great enthusiasm about Pepper, her childhood dog who she was just reminded of. I smirked at Adam. Still pretty sure they'd prefer a dog.

TWELVE

'Miss, if Hamlet's uncle married his mother, does that also make her Hamlet's aunt?' asked Redmond.

Miss Campbell thought about it for a few seconds and shook her head. 'I'm not sure. When I asked for questions on the text, this wasn't really the kind of question I was looking for. Yes, Stephen?'

'Yeah, Miss, but does it?' said Stephen.

We were four weeks into school at this point and the novelty had really worn off. Five days a week of seeing the same dull people proving wrong the teacher's adage that 'there are no stupid questions'. In some ways, I was glad Adam had no friends in school as the prospect of watching him having to engage in conversation with even half of them was grim.

When we first came back, it should be noted that a few of them did make the effort to talk to Adam. The trouble was that either they didn't know what to say to someone they didn't really have a previous relationship with, or they were way too interested in the suicide attempt. There was one kid, Matt, who was constantly asking questions like 'Is there a light at the end of the tunnel?', 'Why a hammer?' or 'Did you see any dead family members or ghost pets?' After a while they stopped talking to Adam beyond making general small talk, either because they were satisfied with the effort they had made, or they had run out of morbid questions.

'Moving forward, the theme that I want you to keep in mind is that of Hamlet's antic disposition. He wants to prove his uncle and aunt's – I mean mother's – deceit, so he pretends to be mad to create a distraction from his investigation. This way if he does anything suspicious, everyone will think "It's just crazy old Hamlet." The question is: is he pretending or is he actually mad?'

The classes themselves were beyond tedious. Maths is boring, Irish is pointless, chemistry is an exercise in watching teenage boys setting their ties on fire with Bunsen burners. Business studies is meh, and besides, I don't see many future captains of industry around me. English I did like, as it was primarily about sitting down and judging things, figuring out what's wrong or right about things and guessing what the writer was thinking. That really appeals to me for some reason. Also Adam was pretty good at it. Perhaps I felt some pride. Oh how sentimental I'm getting now that I'm a few months old.

'Miss?'

'Yes, James?'

'Why are we doing *Hamlet* now? It's only transition year. Leaving Cert isn't for, like, three years.'

'I'm not letting transition year be a complete doss year. If we start preparing today, you'll be more prepared later.'

Have you read *Hamlet*? It's pretty good. Adam and I didn't really understand the language in it but the plot is interesting. We watched a cartoon version of it, but it had lions in it, which are never mentioned in the play, so we watched a longer version with humans, which was really good. A depressed guy and the ghost that tells him to do stuff but he keeps finding excuses not to do it. I can relate.

THIRTEEN

After another week of tolerating the persistent existence of school, we unexpectedly found ourselves at the next weekend. This should have been a relief but it unnerved Adam. He had not seen his new friends since the previous Saturday and had begun to have doubts about their interest in continuing said friendship. He thought it best to not contact them with trivialities in case they would get sick of him too early. However, when they also didn't message him he became convinced that they had probably forgotten about him, so meeting them now would be strange and awkward, and maybe staying in his room and deleting their numbers would be better for all concerned.

However, this situation resolved itself as he was required to leave the house for his session with Dr Moore on Saturday morning, which, of course, meant he would be an audience for Douglas's exit.

Adam sat in the waiting room, worried about the upcoming moment of re-meeting.

'What should I do when Douglas comes in?' he said.

I suggested either a noncommittal hello, enthused reunion, or hiding behind the plant and hoping Douglas didn't see him. But before he could make a decision, Douglas entered the room with his usual confidence and after his obligatory banter with the secretary, he stopped and pointed at Adam.

'You, Hammer,' he said.

'Ah …'

'Sorry, whatever your name is. Adam! – thank you, Dolores – you are required this afternoon. After this interrogation, come to the Merchant's Quay Car Park. Top floor. We need five fine people to achieve a task and you seem like just the man for the job.'

'I don't know, I kinda have–'

'I believe you have mistaken this for a choice. This is not a choice. See you at the car park. Top level.' With that, Douglas walked out the door.

The session with Dr Moore was not especially interesting – it was established that Adam was still finding school a little tough and that he continued to find it difficult to discuss his feelings. After having some lunch, Adam headed to the car park, which was connected to a shopping centre.

'You'll be fine,' I said.

'Easy for you to say, I'm the one who has to act like a normal human being here.'

The top floor of the car park was open air, so you could really appreciate the grey sky. (This place. It's always grey skies.) Leaning over a wall, the foursome already there were staring at the expanse of the city, which also looked grey.

'Hey, Adam,' said Aoife.

'Hey.'

'Excellent, you've arrived. We can begin,' said Douglas.

'So what is the big task?' asked Adam nervously.

'Oh, yes, the plan is to collect five individuals and stand on the roof of a car park,' said Douglas. 'Perhaps we will discuss nonsense. I haven't decided.'

'Top plan,' said Linda.

'Inspired,' said Aoife.

'Oh. Well, I'm never the one to break up a good plan. I guess I can stand in place too,' said Adam, a little relieved that it wasn't some manner of prank that would rely on him doing something cool. He would be unlikely to meet such a challenge.

'Sterling work,' said Douglas.

'Excellent,' said Aoife.

'An asset to the team,' said Linda. 'Actually, since you are here, Barry has a question for you.'

Barry cleared his throat.

'Are you gay?' he said in a practical tone.

'Ah, no.'

'Crap.'

'Sorry.' Adam really regretted disappointing people. I considered this to be an unfortunate trait.

'I'd better explain. Barry is insisting on there being a second gay person in our group before he comes out,' said Linda, who was rolling a cigarette.

'I have my reasons,' Barry said.

'Ridiculous reasons,' sighed Linda.

'You see, if I come out, I'll be the gay one of the group. People will be like "Do you know Barry?" "No" "Oh, you know him. HE IS THE GAY ONE."'

'You prefer to be known as the guy with the dumb jumper he wears every day?' said Linda.

'Yes. Yes, I do,' said Barry, crossing his arms.

'So you're not leaving the closet?'

'Not until we make another gay friend. If there are two of us, it can't be the defining characteristic, so then I can come out.'

'Okay. We could make friends with Alan,' said Aoife.

'Eugh, not Alan. He's a prick.'

'Right. Sinead?'

'No, she's a lesbian. That won't solve anything.'

'Should we make friends with her anyway? She is pretty cool,' said Linda.

'Yes. Yes, we should. But first we need to solve this.'

'I'm not sure if we know any more gay guys, unless … Douglas, did you decide if you were or not?'

'Irrelevant! As you know, I have taken a vow of celibacy in order to fully concentrate on my music, ergo my sexual preference is a meaningless concept and will not be relevant until I later write my autobiography.'

'Adam, are you sure you're not gay? It would be handy.'

Adam shrugged. I didn't think he was gay. (Certain searches on Google I've seen him entering would back up this assertion. Also I noticed that his eyes had a habit of lingering on one of the females in our party a second too long to be completely innocent.) But he was new to the group, so he didn't want to disappoint.

'Well, I guess I can't be sure. Don't they say that sexuality is fluid and–'

'Hey, you kids! I thought I told ye to ged away from it,' shouted a security guard who had just spotted them. He began to walk in our direction so the group decided to move on.

'We want equality! I don't see why only cars can park here. Why not humans?' said Douglas as a parting shot.

And just like that, the gang was back on the street.

'What now?' said Barry.

They thought for a moment in silence.

'Stand outside Lidl?' suggested Aoife.

'Yeah, okay,' said Douglas.

They did so for several hours.

FOURTEEN

Now that Adam's sleep was more regular, I was able to traipse around town on a near nightly basis. Since I had seen what the city looked like during the day, I could appreciate now how different it was at night, the glow of the amber streetlights and the dark river rippling beneath the city. (That said, I had been encouraging Adam to take more naps in the middle of the day so I could go exploring on my own in daylight as well. However, he usually had excuses like 'I have to eat lunch', 'I have to go to school', or 'No, I'm not doing that.')

That Saturday night I decided to go to the Grand Parade, the central street where fast food joints, loud bars and the city library happily coexisted. There was the large fountain, where people gathered to kiss and fight and eat chicken burgers. It was a marvellous, regular sight in my jaunts and featured all kinds of tensions. I was too early though, that evening, as the mad stuff usually happens around 2 a.m., so I was about to leave when I spotted a familiar face.

Turning the corner on Tuckey Street, there was a trio of young guys about Adam's age but dressed older. They moved in a line of three and in the centre was Philip, the guy whose brother had shuffled off this mortal coil. (Having heard so many euphemisms for death in the last couple of months from people talking to him, Adam started making a list of them. That one from *Hamlet* is my favourite, although Adam's favourite is 'snuffed out like a candle'. We stopped compiling when his mother found it, got frightened and told Dr Moore.)

The group passed the fountain and carried on to the end of the street, crossing the bridge there and walking along the river. I had never gone this way before and was surprised to see how dark the road was, despite not being far from the city centre. Eventually they ended up outside a pub, which looked closed though warm music flowed out of its windows.

'You sure they'll serve us?'

'My sister used to go here all the time. They never check, as long as you aren't being obvious about it.'

They opened the door and the leak of music burst out. Inside there was a group of people holding instruments I didn't recognise, playing songs that somehow sounded both jaunty and melancholic. The boys found a small table in the corner, lit only by a candle in an old wine bottle.

'Eugh, Ross, did we have to come for trad night? I want some choons, not "The English killed my dog and now I'm bummed",' said one, who I now recognised as Matt from school, the cheerfully morbid one.

'You wanted a pint. Here we can get one,' said Ross. 'Also, show a bit of respect, man. Men died for Ireland.'

Philip coughed.

'Oh, yeah,' said Ross, who took this as his signal to go to the bar, presumably as he looked the oldest. He ordered three large glasses of dark, black liquid. On TV, teenagers only drank fizzy golden beers if they were drinking at all, so this stuff was new to me. They took a while to pour too. It looked like there were miniature storms inside the glasses as the drinks settled on the bar.

Eventually, when they were done, Ross gathered up the three pints in his hands and set them down on the table, pushing one towards each of his friends.

'To Chris,' he offered.

They clinked their drinks and all took a sup.

'Jesus, Ross. It's like drinking old coffee,' said Matt.

'You get into it. Also, old fellas drink this, so they would never suspect ya.'

Philip took a big gulp. He didn't seem to enjoy it.

'Anyway, Chris was definitely one of the good ones,' said Ross.

Philip paused a moment before responding. 'I remember one summer when we were kids. We were at the beach. He told me to start crying, out of nowhere. He said he would let me play his Nintendo DS or something if I did. So I did. Just wailing like a big baby, while he announced loudly, "I'll get it for you, little brother." Then he ran into the water and swam out to a ball that was just floating out there. He caught it, came back in and gave it to me. "Thanks, Chris?" I said, a bit confused, but then he winked at a girl a few feet away. She smiled and she came over to talk to him.'

'The dog!'

'Who owned the ball?'

'No idea. He got the shift though.'

They burst out laughing, distracting the bearded fellow on the table next to them from his crossword. Philip's laughter began to tremble.

'He was so cool and confident. I don't know why he would …'

'Phil, it's something you can't predict. My uncle committed suicide and he always seemed as happy as can be.'

'I guess.' Philip looked sadly into his pint. Evidently the time for fun stories had ceased.

'It's a bit of an epidemic, isn't it?' said Matt. 'My ma reckons it comes in waves. One person tops himself, other people see it and decide it's a good idea and they do the same thing which leads–'

'Jesus, Matt, shut up,' said Ross.

'Like you had a couple around Cork last year, not far from me actually. It's super scary. Sure there was that Adam guy who tried it at the start of the summer. I asked him about it, but you know him, wouldn't say boo to a mouse. Argh! Why are you kicking my leg?'

'Because I can't reach your head.'

Philip got up and downed the rest of his pint in one go. 'I'm getting another,' he said and walked up to the bar.

'Three Mu–'

'ID.'

'Sorry, I left it at home.'

'Sorry, kid, there's no way I'm serving you. The guards are locking down on this.'

I've seen mourning people in TV shows before. This was

usually the moment all their rage and frustration comes to a boil and they explode at an innocent bystander. Their friends come to hold them back and then they break down in full view of everyone.

This did not happen. Instead he just nodded. 'Eh, I wanted to go home anyway.'

He walked out without telling his two friends and tried to get a taxi. After ten minutes of failing, he gave up and walked all the way back to his house. I remained beside him, watched him text apologies to his friends waiting for their drinks. The entire hour it took to walk home, he just kept looking at his phone. On it, he was searching the Internet for the term 'copycat suicides'.

FIFTEEN

The third stall in the first floor bathroom was occupied, as were all of them. I have no theories on what class preceded this lunch break that would account for five bathroom stalls being completely full, but as it so happened the bowels aligned and Adam was locked out of his lunchtime fortress of solitude.

Once a stall opened, he rushed in. However, his breath of relief was interrupted almost immediately by someone knocking on the door.

'Come on, I'm turtle-heading here,' the voice shouted.

'Coming!'

Adam flushed the toilet and hid his half-eaten sandwich in his pocket. Being caught eating in the toilet was unlikely to do his reputation many favours. He exited and the kid rushed in past him. Looking around, there were a load of students in there, so Adam washed his hands slowly in the hope that they would disappear soon and he could return to his enamel protector. They didn't, however, so for the first time since he came back Adam was going to have to spend his lunch break in the lunchroom.

In my company, Adam had watched quite a few movies about American high schools on his laptop and I have noticed that there is always a bit where the main character – a guileless young white person – walks into the canteen or whatever and the sarcastic student who has randomly befriended him moments earlier (perhaps it's a form of charity they perform) outlines the various cliques that occupy the schools: jocks, cheerleaders, nerds, Goths, stoners – all garden-variety teens. At first our hero is confused and overwhelmed by this strict tribalism, since he came from the one school in movies that doesn't have this, but by the end he finds himself in a group of like-minded people, the attractive girl likes him and everything works out. Hurray!

Adam's school does not work like this.

First, there are no girls and there aren't really any cliques, per se. There are definitely some students more popular than others and some are just definitely assholes (these guys congregate next to the prefab outside), but as far as I can tell everyone else moves fairly smoothly between groups, as if it's one large ocean of blue blazers. This fluidity of people you'd think would make it difficult for Adam to hide, but the opposite was true. Adam was able to keep up the pretence that he had friends since no one thought he was missing from their group. They assumed he belonged to someone but not to them.

So for this lunch break, to avoid detection of being a big loser, he found a large circle of people having a chat and placed himself at the edge, looking in. His presence was acknowledged but the circle did not widen to include him. Adam was content with this arrangement as it involved no interaction on his part. He didn't even have to listen to what was being talked about.

As the circle chatted, Adam finished his sandwich and noticed that there was a new poster on the wall. Drawn like a comic book, it featured a kid in a hoodie standing waist deep in what looked like black quicksand. Above it was written in large red letters: 'Sinking? Ask for Help.'

Adam stared at it.

'What do you think, Adam?' said the principal, who no one had seen step up behind us. This scared most of the circle and they scattered like mice.

'Oh, it's okay,' said Adam.

'So, that's a good thing to remember. Always ask for help,' the principal said, meaningfully.

'Ah, ahem, why are these up?' said Adam.

'Oh, we thought it would be a good idea after what happened with Chris. Two incidents in a row like that ... we have to start being more careful about our students' mental health.'

'I don't think it's contagious,' said Adam with a surprising edge to his voice, which the principal ignored.

'Not at all what we're suggesting. We just are now aware that your particular problem is not so particular. In fact, since you appear to have made great strides within yourself, you may be excited to hear about our new event.'

Adam seemed less than thrilled. 'New event?'

'Yes, we are organising a day of talks and initiatives on mental health. We want to really reach out with some helpful advice.'

'I recommend not trying to kill yourself with a hammer.'

The principal tutted. 'Humour is important, Adam. I can see that. But I think it would be more helpful to show the rest of the student body that you are a survivor and that suicide is a bad idea, instead of making jokes about how not to do it.'

'Sure,' said Adam, with a slight blush.

Just then the bell rang. Lunch was over and we could escape.

As they had spoken, I had noticed a minor detail on the poster. Some wit had written the words ADAM ON HIS WAY TO MEET CHRIS with an arrow pointing at the half-submerged boy. I thought it best not to mention it.

***

Sitting and listening, and more sitting and writing, each hour identical to the last. God, why must this whole school business persist? The monotony was driving me mad. We were in the science lab after lunch, which at least looked different from the rest of the classrooms and provided opportunities to look at fire.

'Did you watch *Arrow* last night? It was awesome,' said Greasy, his lab partner.

'No, I don't watch that show.'

'You should. It's awesome. Shit, look who's in. Thought he wouldn't be back for ages.'

It was Philip, surrounded by classmates artlessly avoiding

the subject of his absence. He played along, however, laughing and joking as if nothing was different.

'Blah blah blah bla-blah?' said Greasy.

'What?' (Neither of us was listening.)

'Do you have the pipette?' Greasy repeated, with his hand out.

'Oh, yeah, sure.'

The lab continued without incident – well, this was not strictly true; there may have been a small explosion – and Greasy and Adam got the result they were looking for, after some creative recording of measurements. When the bell rang, most people got up and left, except one, who stood on the other side of Adam's countertop.

'Hey, how's it going?' said Greasy, but Philip did not pull his glare from Adam. Adam was glued to the spot, unable to speak. His left foot vibrated violently.

'Eh, good to see you back in school, Phil,' Greasy finished. 'See ya later, Adam.'

Philip's eyes narrowed and, once Greasy was out of sight, he leaned over the desk and pushed his finger into Adam's chest. 'Chris is your fault,' he said, then walked away.

Adam's breath quickened and, as soon as the coast was clear, he quickly ran to the bathroom and hid in his usual stall. After twenty minutes he slowly opened the door and made his way to geography, mumbling something about being called to the office for something. The teacher nodded and told him what page the rest of the class was on. Adam dutifully turned to the right page but I could sense that he wasn't concentrating on the exciting world of oxbow lakes right at that moment.

***

Once home, Adam said little, speaking just enough so that his parents wouldn't be alarmed. Clearly Philip's little jab had wounded him. It was plainly consuming his every thought. This was frustrating, since it meant I would have to suffer through a never-ending set of panic attacks. Nice one, Phil! Now he would go back to spending forever in his room, which meant I would have to spend forever in there too.

Just after dinner, as expected, Adam retreated to his room. I tried to lighten his mood. 'Hey, there's no need to be upset. It's not your fault Phil blames you.'

'But why does he blame me?'

'Oh, he probably thinks you inspired his brother to do the deed.'

'Is that a thing? Bleurgh.'

He moved to his desk and sat there.

'Wha cha doing?' I said, in my friendly voice. (I'm not a big fan of my friendly voice. It's a bit high.)

'Nothing,' he said tersely.

He truly was doing nothing. He sat stiffly, his concentration focused on the water stain in the corner of the ceiling. (It still looked like half a bicycle.)

'Alright,' I said. 'Um … do you have homework to do?'

Finally he looked at the clock, sighed heavily and pulled out some sheets of paper from his bag. He began writing something down, then dropped his pen and then his head.

I looked over his shoulder and saw a paragraph about a girl on a bed. What was this?

'I have to write this dumb story for tomorrow,' he said. Apparently I was not paying attention in class when his English teacher had given out this assignment. Making up stories was homework?

'What do you have so far?'

He lifted his arm to reveal that the visible paragraph was in fact the only paragraph. I reread it. It was about a person lying hopelessly in bed. I liked it and said as much. This brightened him up.

'Don't know where to go with it, though. I want to write something sad, mostly cos I feel too shitty to write anything else,' he said.

I stared at it. Something sad was forming in my head as an idea.

'I have something,' I said. 'Do you want it?'

'Please.'

I told him.

'I like it!' he said. 'It's kinda grim, but I think we could do this.'

And thus we started. We worked together solidly for the next hour and in the end we had a two-page story. He looked at it with some satisfaction and I will confess I did too. It was a particular feeling, like I had briefly forgotten my main purpose of making snarky comments for my own benefit and found another.

'Oh wait, there is a theme we were supposed to follow,' Adam said. He looked through his schoolbag and pulled out a black journal. He pointed at an entry from that week.

'Oh, that's kind of the opposite of what we wrote.'

We mulled for a moment and decided on a last line that would tie it in perfectly.

5/10/17 ADAM MURPHY

A GOOD BOOK

Emily lay at the edge of the bed and looked sadly at the hairy whale snoring beside her. He had fallen asleep almost immediately after the transaction. He slept on his back, his stomach a perpetually ~~expanding~~ bloating and shrinking balloon.

Emily sat up and looked at the clock on the night stand. It said it was 11.52, nearly midnight. ~~He had her for the whole night.~~ He had paid for the whole night so no point in checking. She wished nothing more than to not be there. She wasn't sure exactly how she ended up in that room. Once, she was just a girl sitting on her own bed, surrounded by posters of horses. Now she was sitting on some hotel's bed, surrounded by nothing.

~~Did she need to wait the full hour?~~ Did she need to hang around? It looked like he was asleep for the night. I guess he paid up and some customers get weird about her leaving early. To occupy herself, she began to look through the drawers of the nightstand.

Inside the bottom drawer there was a Bible. A friend of hers, Debbie, a while ago, was obsessed with hotel Bibles. She used to be in hotels a lot for a reason Emily couldn't remember. Her dad was an hotelier, maybe? She once explained in great detail that the Bibles weren't the hotel's. Instead they were left by a group of monks known as the Gideon Order. They liked to travel around a lot and whichever rooms they stayed in, they made sure to leave behind them a small brown book, bound in fake leather, in case the lonely or remorseful are trapped in a hotel room (much like this desperate situation).

And then her friend Debbie explained that there ~~was~~ were stories that these same monks occasionally left money in between some of the pages to reward those who turn to God. Nothing too big, maybe a tenner, although maybe sometimes there was word of a 50 dollar note haunting the pages.

Emily thought of this story and lifted the Bible. It was not heavy. She thought to herself, 'If it's true, if monks travel the world, leaving money … if I open this book and find 20 dollars, I'll take it as a sign that I should not be here. I'll spend it on a bus ticket and go home, if not home, somewhere else. Somewhere for me.'

A whole life opened before her eyes, one of green fields and cute shops and sunny skies.

She opened the book and flicked through the pages.

Nothing. It was empty. It was just a stupid story.

She put the book back, lay down on the bed and listened to the sound of passing trucks and wondered where they were going.

She checked the clock again. It was 12.01. 'Happy birthday to me,' she said as she turned sixteen.

SIXTEEN

'Miss, I think Hamlet is definitely crazy since he wants to have sex with his mam and that's manky,' said Mingsy. Uff, everyone in this place has a stupid nickname.

'An astute observation, Michael,' said Miss Campbell. 'There is certainly evidence of an Oedipal complex which may be clouding his judgement. Can anyone else point to other signifiers that suggest Hamlet's antic disposition isn't pretence?'

We were at the point where Hamlet was putting on a play to reveal his uncle's guilt, which seemed very elaborate to me. Personally I felt he knew that Claudius was guilty and was just using it as an excuse to dabble in theatre. The bell rang.

'Ah, I wasn't paying attention to the time,' said Miss Campbell. 'Okay, everyone make sure that you read Act Three for tomorrow. There will be questions. Oh, and Adam? Could you hang on?'

As the rest of the students vacated the room for their next class, Adam approached her desk. She was designated the 'good-looking' one of the female teachers in the school (or 'a total ride' as Mingsy called her), though it would appear she didn't appreciate being the object of adolescent desire, judging by her eye roll when Mingsy nudged Adam on the way out and winked.

'Yes, Miss?' he said with some dread. He was fairly confident that Miss Campbell was not about to start an illicit affair with him, so this could only be because of his story. Perhaps it was too risqué and gritty for St Jude's delicate sensibilities.

'I read your story, Adam,' she said with some weight.

Adam was gripped with fear. 'Oh, sorry about that. I guess I shouldn't be writing about–'

'No need to say sorry at all!' she said with surprise. 'Other than a few sentences that were a little off grammatically, I thought it was very good. I'm actually a bit surprised. I didn't realise that you could write creatively. All your stuff before now was fine, but this, this shows real potential. It has a rare empathy.'

This was our first critical review and a generally positive one too, although I did wonder which were the 'off' sentences she was referring to. They must have been pretty obvious; otherwise she wouldn't have mentioned it. I knew we shouldn't have included that bit about the horses. Adam was relieved though.

'Thanks, Miss!' he said. 'I'm glad you liked it. Ah, is that all?'

Miss Campbell pulled out her wallet and opened it. I thought she was going to pay us for writing such a good story, but it was soon clear that there was no money in there, just loose papers and receipts where euro notes should be.

'I realise you have had … personal troubles recently,' she said, as she searched the debris, 'but creative writing can be a great way to express yourself and perhaps work through some issues.'

'Oh.'

'Or fun. It can be fun! No issues resolved. It's just I think you may have something worth exploring. Ah, here it is!'

From a small pocket, she pulled out a small collection of dog-eared cards and presented one to Adam. It said in big lettering 'YOUNG WRITERS ASSEMBLE! Creative writing workshops for teenagers', and, in smaller detail, the place and time. It was on after school on Fridays.

'I think it could be seriously beneficial for your writing, if it's something you wish to pursue. Do you know where the Unitarian Church is?'

'The one where all the hippies sell stuff outside?'

'That's the one.'

Adam looked at the card. 'Ah, thanks, Miss,' he said uncertainly.

'Go on so,' she said, seemingly cheered that she may have discovered a new literary light.

***

I don't know much about history's greatest writers but I understand that they drew their inspiration from their surroundings, so it's probably important to find inspiring surroundings: sweeping countryside, cool cafés, jungles. There's most likely a list somewhere on the Internet ('34 places to write your masterpiece'), but I strongly suspect that not listed is the back room of a small Unitarian church in Cork, Ireland.

'This is the place,' said Adam when we stood outside the

Princes Street building, hidden like a dormouse between a Starbucks and a hardware store. We walked down the paved path, passing engravings of worship. Inside was a modest building and the sound of chatter led us to the back quarters where a circle of would-be scribes were seated. The timbers of the wooden floors echoed with a large clunk on every step, so everyone was immediately aware of Adam's arrival. They all turned around and stared at the newcomer.

'Adam!' said a familiar voice. It was Aoife.

'Thank God,' he muttered.

'This would be a good place to do it,' I said, looking at the cross on the wall. 'You'll be pretty covered.'

Ignoring me, Adam found a stool and pushed it next to Aoife, much to the ire of the pasty gentleman next to her.

'Hey! I didn't know you write things,' she said.

'I don't … well, I guess, I'm starting to. My teacher, Miss Campbell, suggested it.'

'Miss Campbell? Oh, you mean Niamh?'

Miss Campbell (or *Niamh*, apparently) entered, holding some sheets and a selection of mismatched pens.

'Great to see you here, Adam. Time for writing!'

This received a big whoop from the circle. They must really be into writing.

***

Writing exercises are weird. First Miss Campbell – I mean

Niamh – asked the group to write down a list of their favourite places in the world. We weren't to think about it, just write down what came naturally. Adam started and had pretty big trouble thinking of places he liked. After three minutes, he had his room, the park near his house and Coney Island (which was a fairground on a beach in New York he has never visited, but which looked cool in pictures). He looked over at Aoife, whose list was reaching the end of the page.

'Okay, stop,' Miss Campbell said. 'Now I want you to think of people from history. They can be good or bad. Just write them down.'

Our list (I helped out on this one) of famous historical people was a bit longer: Michael Collins, Hitler, Abraham Lincoln and Oscar Wilde all made appearances.

'Okay, stop!' she said. 'I want you now to take the last favourite place on your list and the last person on your other list and start writing something with both of them in it.'

Adam looked at his lists. It was going to have to be a story about Julius Caesar in a famous amusement park. Adam looked up and could see that everyone else had already started writing.

'Just start writing,' whispered Aoife. 'It's not a test.'

He put pen to paper and began: *Returning the conquering hero, Caesar had seized Gaul and Britain, and to celebrate, he went to Coney Island. It was time to conquer his great fear, the WonderWheel …*

***

Afterwards, Adam and Aoife walked together to the side of the street deemed the easiest to be picked up from.

'Soooooo, can I read what you wrote?' asked Aoife, as they waited.

'Ah, I'd prefer if you didn't.'

'Well, if it's too personal … I mean, the class is only for expressing yourself and all.'

Adam laughed. The laugh was rather easy, with a lightness I was unfamiliar with. 'Yeah, I'm not sure you can handle my deep thoughts about stuff,' he said, handing her the sheets of paper on which he had scribbled.

'These are insightful. Excellent, but insightful too,' she said, trying to hide a smile. On the sheets of paper, Adam had written two paragraphs and then had drawn several doodles of rabbits. They weren't very good so I'm assuming that Aoife's approval was nothing more than politeness.

'Now that you know too much about me, can I see what you wrote?'

'Sure.'

Aoife pulled out her neat leather journal and pulled from it two neatly folded pieces of paper, that were folded with the corners touching each other perfectly.

'I'm not going to show you what I wrote tonight, because it's terrible, but here's something I wrote earlier.'

'Two pages, double-sided?'

'It's too late now. You're committed.'

Adam made a sad expression, biting his bottom lip. Aoife

grinned as if she had walked in on something embarrassing. It was clear to me that they were engaging in some obscure communication I was unfamiliar with.

'You don't have to read it if you really don't want to.'

'No, no. I want to.'

In front of them, a car beeped and a hand waved from behind the wheel.

'Ah, there's my dad. See you tomorrow!' she said, hopping into the car.

'See ya!'

'ALSO REMEMBER IF YOU DON'T LIKE IT, I'LL HATE YOU FOREVER,' she shouted out the window, as the car drove by.

'Hey, Adam,' said his mother, who had appeared right behind him, making him jump slightly. 'I had to park by the School of Music. Who's your friend?'

'Oh, just someone I know,' said Adam.

'Of course,' said Mum, smiling. There was a lot of smiling that night. On the way home, he held up his phone to the page so that he could read Aoife's story. It was pretty weird and I didn't really get the jokes, but Adam seemed to enjoy it. When we arrived home, he decided to start writing something immediately. The class was clearly more inspiring than I had thought.

CHANGES

by Aoife Tuffour-Callaghan

DRAFT 2ish

The vampire bared his nude teeth. Anne pulled her hair away to reveal her neck, expertly made up to emphasise what she presumed was her juiciest vein. Soon she would be the eternal lover of the vampire; how thrilling to lose one's mortality in the local grave-yard.

He plunged his terrible fangs into her and drank. In response, she moaned. (A little too loudly, she thought. She didn't want him to think that she was one of those girls. He seemed old-fashioned.)

The vampire grabbed her hand and, with her sharpest nail, he carved a line in his breast and entreated her to suckle on his wound. Anne thought for a moment what her family would think of her participation in this unholy parody of the mother feeding her newborn. But it was for the briefest of moments, as she quickly obliged.

At first, the iron taste repelled her, but after a few sups of crimson, it became richer and full of ghastly life, replacing her deceased purity with a new demonic brew.

'Done!' announced the vampire, gently pushing away Anne's head from his ivory chest.

'What?' said Anne, wiping a trickle of blood from her mouth.

'Done. You are a vampire now.'

Anne licked the errant haemoglobin off her index finger. 'That was surprisingly quick.'

The vampire shrugged and then pulled out a shopping bag from behind the gravestone of Arthur C. Chesterfield. He checked inside it first, removed a packet of crisps and handed it to Anne. Anne looked inside to find what looked like curtains.

'Go on, put it on. I guessed you are a size ten.'

Anne pulled it out. It was a nightie, made of heavy cloth.

'Eh ... thank you, but this is not really ...'

The vampire became crestfallen.

'... something I've worn before. So naturally I'm very excited to put this on as soon as possible.'

'Great! There is a crypt over there you can change in. Don't worry, I won't peek,' said the vampire.

'I don't really mind if you watch ...' Anne began to say but stopped due to the vampire's schoolboy giggles. She took the bag and walked through the iron gates of the tomb.

'You know, it's a bit cold tonight. Can I change at the castle?'

'You're a vampire now! Everything is cold.'

'Oh, I didn't realise that.'

Anne entered the stone building and laid the nightie on the stone slab in the centre. She then removed her jeans, T-shirt, cardigan and shoes and put on her new costume. It was a unique combination of drafty and claustrophobic. She pulled a compact mirror from her jeans pocket. Turned out the old legend about vampires' lack of reflections was not a lie.

'Oh, someone is a mistress of suspense,' shouted the vampire from outside.

Anne stepped out to reveal herself to him and was rewarded with the sound of a swoon and a selection of highly complimentary adjectives.

Anne could only guess what her undead beau considered attractive, but it was most likely for the best that mirrors did not work.

'But no longer shall we delay! To the castle, for I have wicked plans for the night!'

Anne breathed a sigh of relief, expelling the remaining air in her useless lungs. Sure he was fussy about looks, but now the fantasy could continue to the large cavernous threshold, built for misdeeds not suitable for human eyes.

'I purchased New Moon on audio book. Naughty times!'

Anne scratched her head.

'But after … we will … you know …'

The vampire with a sweeping hand picked up Anne by her waist and drew her close. He placed her hand on his breast, the fingers trembling at record speeds.

'Feel that heartbeat?' he whispered into her ear. She waited a few moments and felt no pulse.

'No …'

He released her. 'Well, there you go. No blood flow. Ain't nothing happened since 1893,' he said pointing downward.

'So I have committed myself to an eternity of really serious hickeys.'

'Indeed, but probably not tonight. I still feel quite full.'

Anne's mother was right. Never get involved with a vampire, she had said.

The vampire looked around, his cape lifting and falling in the slight breeze.

'I don't know this area at all. Do you have a number for a cab?' he said.

SEVENTEEN

Parents, much like elephants, never forget, and also, like elephants, are not terribly subtle. The next evening dinner conversation no longer focused on school (which Adam was perfectly happy with and I was no less delighted by, having stood by for the last month and a half listening to made-up assurances that school was going fine). Instead Mum had nothing but questions about the writing group. It was clear to me what she wanted to know, but Adam's mum was cunning. She knew that she would not get the information she wanted by directly asking. Her initial questions were general: What was he writing? What was his teacher like? What do the other people write? She asked these for over a half hour and, since his father was late due to going away drinks for Harry from work, there was no one to deflect to.

An unsuspecting Adam answered her questions truthfully, wandering into the trap.

'So what kind of things does your friend write?' she said.

'My friend?'

'The girl I saw you talking to.'

'Oh, Aoife. Funny stuff with vampires in it.'

Mum considered this information and phrased her next question carefully. 'I'm surprised she's called Aoife. Do you know where she's from?'

'Oh, Ballincollig, I think.'

'Really? She looked … never mind. I suppose it's rude to ask.'

'Why are you asking?'

'No reason. I'm just glad you are making friends at your group,' she said, before dropping the topic. She followed up with a discussion about a mix-up at work that day that led to her accidentally reporting that a beloved musician had died.

Later, while Adam was watching TV, his father walked in and sat down next to him. Interactions with Adam's father were generally brief. However their relationship was engineered, it did not allow for conversations longer than ten minutes. After the ten minutes were up, they would both resume staring at the closest available screen.

'Your mother tells me you're making friends.'

'She did seem very interested at dinner.'

'She mentioned a girl in particular.'

'I don't really want to have this conversation.'

'Now, she just wanted me to reassure you that we are much more cosmopolitan than you would think. Before I met your mother, I dated an English girl, which at the time–'

'Please stop. A, she is from Ballincollig and B, the reason I haven't mentioned her is because there is nothing to mention. She's just my friend.'

'Sure. No rush. We're right here for when you want to talk.'

We had heard this sentence before, except this time it was different. Before, it was filled with fear, like slowly opening a box full of snakes; this time it sounded more pleased, like quickly opening a box of fun things that aren't snakes. It occurred to me that this was the first time in a long time they had had an issue with their son that was a normal boy problem – in fact one of the most common of problems: romance.

Adam smiled to himself. Whatever his intentions were towards Aoife, he liked being the centre of attention for reasons other than being Mr Attempted-Suicide.

After he and his dad watched half an episode of *Friends*, the one where Joey's fridge is broken, he excused himself and went to his bedroom.

'Should we write?' he said.

'Sure.'

The story we had started the previous day was half done, so it made sense to continue with that. I was finding writing a most satisfying experience, I guess because it functions as my only means of communication beyond Adam, who wasn't the most exciting audience. We had worked out a system. Adam would suggest something. I'd tell him his idea was dreadful, explain how I would improve it, we'd have a little argument and then move forward. It was a flawless story delivery system. We hadn't decided on an ending yet, but Adam was insistent that we finish it soon, that night even. I wasn't clear on why there was such a rush, but I agreed.

This story was about a guy who looks out the window and notices the nearby wood is getting closer and closer each day. This freaks him out, so he tells the neighbours but they don't believe him, telling him he is mad. He decides the trees must be moving at night when he's asleep, so he drinks a lot of coffee so that he can stay awake and see them move. However, he falls asleep and when he wakes up it's still dark outside. He looks out but he can't see the trees in the darkness. He checks his watch. It says it's the middle of the day.

The trees have reached the house and are blocking out the light.

EIGHTEEN

It took a while for Adam to get used to the idea that he had friends. Instead of watching a movie, he was able to go, 'Hey, I wonder what the gang is up to. I should join them in this activity.' We weren't sure how it happened either. It was like he walked around a corner without looking where he was going and slammed into the Famous Five. The movies and TV shows we watched suggested that becoming friends with people involved a long list of favours, or pretending to become friends for some strategic advantage, or being born next door to some doe-eyed, brown-haired gal. I think Adam was particularly confused, although, to be fair, he didn't have many friends before, so he had no experience to compare it to.

One day, after school, they were all hanging out in a Subway and Adam asked how the rest of them had become friends. They provided a convoluted oral history, which I present to you now completely unedited:

Barry: 'I dunno. I think we all just stood in one place on Paul Street and eventually we ended up speaking to each other.'
Aoife: 'No, wait, I knew Linda from dance class.'
Linda: 'Oh, that's right! Our mothers had serious notions of us becoming great dancers. We were to be the next … whoever is a famous ballerina. We started talking when we fell into each other attempting a simultaneous pirouette.'

Aoife: 'I was not the graceful swan I was led to believe I was by my mother.'

Linda: 'We giggled so much that the dance instructor sent us to the dressing room for a full fifteen minutes. Anyway, afterwards, Aoife was being picked up by her very attractive older brother. So there and then, I made it my business to make friends with her.'

Aoife: 'She was not subtle about it.'

Linda: 'I was not.'

Aoife: 'He was frightened.'

Linda: 'He misunderstood my intentions.'

Aoife: 'You stole his hamster.'

Linda: 'Correction: I borrowed his hamster. I thought he would naturally fall in love with the woman who rescued his beloved pet.'

Aoife: 'We put up Missing posters and all for it.'

Douglas: 'Then I entered in a triumph.'

Linda: 'What?'

Douglas: 'I'm sorry to derail this unsettling tale of attempted hamstercide—'

Linda: 'Hey! It was at most a hamsternapping.'

Douglas: '… but this origin story has been going on for a long time without getting to the real meat of the legend – when I deigned to become friends with you. You see, it all began in Madagascar.'

Linda: 'Douglas lives in the same park as me. So when Aoife and I started hanging out here, being the cool chicks that we are, Douglas naturally gravitated to us.'

Douglas: 'That is not how I remember it. It all goes back to three years ago … the summer everything changed.'

Barry: 'I literally was just sitting outside Burritos and Blues and they filled the other three seats one day.'

Douglas: 'Barry, it was friendship at first sight. Why must you question these things?'

So in answer to the original question, I somehow had even less clue as to how people make friends. But then their chosen hunting ground, Paul Street, was home to many miscellaneous groups. Populated by kids with dyed hair, dark clothes, skateboards and loud laughs, it was a home from home, one filled with floating emos and weirdos.

Down the edges of Paul Street was a little street and an empty alleyway. The alleyway proved popular with teens who had procured bottles of alcohol and other things, and couples who snuck away from their groups to eat each other's faces. When we passed such things, Adam always looked away shyly, perhaps fearing that if they caught his eye he would suddenly plunge into a world of illicit sex and drugs without warning. He seemed so easily frightened by this that I told him he was destined never to have a girlfriend.

I was wrong about that, as it turned out.

NINETEEN

Dr Moore sat back in his seat. He had replaced the hideous painting of a horse with a worse one featuring a giraffe on a beach.

'Adam, how was this week?' he asked.

Adam shrugged. 'It was all right.'

'How are you feeling about school at the moment. Okay?'

Adam sighed. 'Grand,' he said. 'I'm not super enjoying it but I've stopped hiding in the fortress of solitude at lunchtime.'

'The what?'

'Oh, the toilet. The fortress of solitude is where Superman goes when he wants to hang out on his own.'

'I see. I was always more of a Spiderman fan. Have you had any success with your classmates?'

'Not really. They don't seem to hate me or anything ...'

Well, that's not quite true for all of them, I reminded him.

'... but I've made some friends outside of school. Actually one of them is Douglas, the kid before me here.'

'Oh, yes,' Dr Moore said, a bit too unsurprised.

'That sounds like you talked about me. Did you talk about me?'

'Sorry, I can't discuss other people's sessions. How did you become friends?'

'Ah ... he just seemed to decide one day that we were and

I didn't disagree.'

'I'm not surprised. He is a charismatic young man.'

'Also I joined a writing group and one of his friends, Aoife, goes too. I guess she is one of my friends now as well. We swap stories and stuff.'

I noticed a note of interest on Dr Moore's face.

'Can you tell me more about Aoife?'

'Oh, she is really cool. She's a Goth, but she was telling me that since her mother is from South Africa that means she is an Afrogoth, and she writes these really funny stories with monsters and vampires and things like that. She listens to really terrible music, though. I tried listening to it a couple of times, and she has a load of different genres like grindcore, industrial, but they have no tune or …'

Adam went on about her for a solid five additional minutes before finally getting to his other friends.

'This is very promising,' Dr Moore said. 'How does it feel to have friends?'

'Good, I think,' said Adam.

'You think?'

'Well, I'm a little worried, to be honest. I've had friends before and they all kind of disappeared over time. What if these guys get bored too?'

'Adam, you're not boring.'

'Yeah, I know but–'

'No buts. Concentrate on the positives. They have invited you to be their friend.'

'Got it,' Adam said, 'but people change their minds, you know?'

TWENTY

'OH, COME ON SHEPPARD!' Douglas shouted with a degree of irritation. 'IT WAS WIDE OPEN!'

Adam sat next to Douglas in the stand, eating what must have been quickly cooling chips. The lights beamed on the pitch, while players scrambled over each other to kick a wet ball. This was a soccer game.

The reason we were here was simply that Douglas had rung Adam earlier that day. It should be noted that Douglas never messaged, only rang. This was due to his principled stand against the mobile phone, so he was relegated to using the landline. I wasn't sure why Adam's house had a landline (the only two people who rang Adam's landline were his aunt and Douglas), but I have been assured they were very popular in the past.

The conversation had gone something like this:

'Adam, do you like soccer?'

'Well, I–'

'Glad to hear it. I will see you at the entrance to the Cross, tonight at seven.'

Douglas hung up.

'I guess I am going to see some soccer,' Adam said.

'You gave in easily there,' I said.

'Ah, you know. It might be fun. Also I kinda owe him.'

He said no more but I knew what he meant. Douglas,

brash and weird as he was, had essentially given him a new set of friends, a new life for seemingly little in return and no obvious motivation, so Adam was inclined to go along with whatever he said. This minimised the risk of losing it all.

Anyway, it would be a new experience for me. Adam never watched any sports so I only knew of it from hearing snatches of conversation in the schoolyard, or from the occasional glimpse on TV before his father changed the channel.

'So soccer is the egg ball one?' I asked.

***

After Adam gave me a brief explanation of what sounded like a needlessly complex way of kicking a ball, and when we figured out where 'the Cross' was, his mum gave us a lift. She was equally confused about why Adam would suddenly wish to watch a soccer match and gave him ample warning on how cold the stadium got these nights.

Douglas was standing outside wearing a long red and white scarf. 'Hi, Adam, here's my grandad's season ticket,' he said. 'Try to look more retired.'

Adam made a coughing noise. 'Hello, Sonny Jim, I'm Douglas's grandpapa,' he said in a cracked voice.

Douglas did not laugh.

Entering the toll booth, the woman said, 'Hello, Douglas.' Then she looked at Adam's card, stifled a laugh and motioned us through.

Inside the gates were mountains of people dressed in big jackets and similar scarves to Douglas. We were seated on one side of the pitch. We waited as the announcements told us who was playing and which sponsors we could thank. It began to rain.

'I didn't know you were into football,' said Adam.

'Evidently I am. Just Cork City though, I'm not one for attaching your hopes and dreams to tedious millionaires in London. Also, don't call it football, we're not English.'

'Oh, yeah. That makes sense.'

'Do you follow any teams?'

'I wouldn't say I'm a big fan but I keep an eye on it,' said Adam. I would like to emphasise that that day was the first time Adam had ever mentioned football.

A man in a pink shirt blew a whistle and the game began. On one side of the pitch a crowd noisily chanted songs which I'm fairly confident didn't mention Cork City in the original lyrics. The game was quite something to watch. The ball bounced up and down the pitch, accompanied by whoops and boos.

Feeling out of place, Adam kept forgetting to stand up when the ball came close to a goal, and clapped whenever something happened, including when the opposite team gained control of the ball, which he soon learned from the displeased expressions of those around him was a no-no. Douglas didn't seem to notice, though, as he was very much into the game. Gone was the cool dude who would make great statements with a flourish; instead he was tense and passionate, shouting and cheering as the match wore on.

Around a half hour in, something rang. It wasn't Adam's phone, in fact it was coming from Douglas's pocket.

'Dammit! She is always doing this to me. Sneaking this contraption onto my person when I'm not looking.'

'Who's she? Your mum?'

'Yes, my mother. Hello, dear! Yes, I do know what night it is. I'm at a match. I don't care if I need to practise. WHAT WAS THAT, KEEPER?! Yes, I was referring to you!'

Douglas flung the phone from his hand without looking, hitting the man with the flag in the back of the head.

'It slipped,' he said, as the flag man threw it back to him.

'What was that all about?' I said to Adam, who I knew would be too timid to ask.

'That was one of my jailers,' said Douglas, without being asked. 'Apparently I forgot to go to a vital piano lesson this evening, as if Cork versus Dundalk is somehow less vital than me banging the same few keys over and over.'

Adam said nothing but nodded his head.

'"Your Christmas exams are in three months. You should be looking at college courses, you are wasting your talents … mah mah mah." Well, they are my talents to waste! Besides, the leaving cert isn't for another three years.'

Adam was struck dumb, so instead of responding, he worried at the programme Douglas had handed him earlier. Douglas's fingers rapped the back of the seat in front of him.

'Do you have this problem, Adam?'

'What problem?'

'People expecting things. They spend their whole life telling you that they expect great things from you and then they are annoyed when they decide you're not giving them what they require. My Bs are as good as anyone else's, but apparently not good enough for my parents. They expect better.'

'I really don't think people expect much from me,' said Adam.

'Lucky you.'

Suddenly the crowd exploded. I guess there was finally a goal. Douglas jumped up with joy and Adam joined him, delighted to be relieved of the conversation.

***

By the end of the game, Douglas was in better form. Cork's 2–1 victory buoyed him and he seemed unusually lighthearted. This all disappeared once he stepped outside.

'You want a lift, Adam?' he said, his offer sounding surprisingly irritated.

A tall, thin man in an impeccable dark suit was standing by the stadium gate. 'Douglas,' he said, 'who is your friend? I don't believe we've had the pleasure of meeting.'

'It's Adam, Father. Adam, this is my father.'

'Oh yes,' said his father, 'Douglas has mentioned you.' His eyes dashed to Adam's forehead. Adam's fringe was hiding the scar remarkably well. You really needed to look for it.

'Oh, eh, it's always good to be talked about,' said Adam.

'Indeed. As Wilde said, the only thing worse than being talked about—'

'He needs a lift,' said Douglas, interrupting.

'Well, if it's not inconvenient,' Adam added quickly.

'It's no trouble at all,' said Douglas's dad tersely.

They walked to a car parked close by. It was an impressive one. If I knew anything about cars, I would describe its metal beauty in all its glory, but sorry, reader, it's a gap in my knowledge.

Adam told Douglas's father his address, who then typed it into his GPS machine on the dashboard. He said with satisfaction, 'Your house is on our way. How nice.'

We drove for a few minutes before 'Father' attempted to start a conversation, much to everyone's regret. 'How was the match?'

'It was good, Mr …' Adam realised he didn't know Douglas's second name.

'Cork won,' finished Douglas.

'That's good,' he said. 'If you had skipped your music lesson for a loss, it would have been a waste.'

'I could have skipped my lesson for three hours of standing on hot coals and it still wouldn't have been a bigger waste of time than more classes with that bore.'

'Luckily, we were able to reschedule to this weekend,' said his father, ignoring him.

'Woop-di-do.'

'Adam, I must apologise for Douglas. I would prefer if he kept his snide comments to a time when we don't have company.'

'That's fine. I didn't really–'

'There is no need to apologise. Adam is quite a fan of my snide comments.'

'I sincerely doubt that. I can only imagine he finds them quite tiresome, just like the rest of us do.'

'Well, Adam?'

'Eh, I think this is my stop.'

'Oh, yes,' said Douglas's father.

'Thank you,' said Adam, as the car slowed down.

'Goodnight.'

'See you later.'

They drove off. Adam and I looked at each other and, in unison, said, 'That was awkward.'

TWENTY-ONE

What horrors, it was poetry night in the Unitarian church. Adam was using his evening with Douglas for the purposes of 'ART'. His poem so far was a collection of half sentences about the night that Cork City met Dundalk. (At least I think it was a poem, it didn't rhyme or anything.) I had no interest in poetry so I left him to compose by himself.

Aoife was scribbling away as usual into one of her notebooks, using her seeming ability to turn the writing instinct on and plough ahead. She never seemed to pause to think even about a sentence. It was like she was writing automatically. (Not to be confused with Automatic Writing, a Victorian practice of communicating with the dead by letting your hands be possessed by a spirit and writing whatever came. Adam and I tried it once after reading about it on the Internet. He wrote 'armadillo'. I definitely didn't suggest this as I don't know what one is.)

Adam looked at his hastily assembled words and decided to give Aoife a poke.

'Ah, can I ask you something?'

'I believe there is no law against it … yet,' said Aoife, who didn't look up from her writing.

'What's the story with Douglas?'

'I hope you two are comparing poetry notes,' said *Niamh*. I still found her different names weird, especially as she seemed much more relaxed in this class than her school one. She was also sassier and made more jokes.

'Yes, Miss, I mean Niamh!'

Aoife laughed. She had a light laugh. 'What do you mean?'

'Well, I was at a footba–'

'Say no more. We've all been to *that* football game.'

'Really?'

Aoife nodded her head sagely. 'Douglas has a few issues with his parents.'

'Are they awful to him? I met his dad and he seemed fine, if a little aloof.'

'It's not that. Well, I don't know. I've never met them. What I think is … well, I think Douglas is very highly strung and tries to cover it by being Douglas.'

Adam was baffled, as was I. Out of the grab-bag of friends Adam had found himself, Douglas seemed the closest to the cool kids on TV.

'See, I think Douglas is really smart,' said Aoife. 'Like really, really smart, so his parents expect him to do great things.'

'Oh,' said Adam. His expression suggested that he agreed with what Aoife had just said, even though it made no sense.

'You should ask Barry about the time he saw Cork City versus Shamrock Rovers with Douglas. He still does the sign of the cross to this day!'

'Time's up!' said Niamh. 'Would anyone like to read their poem? I know how much you young people enjoy volunteering for things.'

Aoife shifted in her seat a little too visibly.

'Aoife?'

'Oh ah … I think Adam said he wanted to go first.'

'I didn't!'

'Excellent! Adam, work away.'

Aoife smiled a wicked grin at Adam. What a horrible thing to do. Obviously I was quite impressed.

Adam stood up nervously. All that was on his sheet were the few scribbled fragments he had before he interrupted Aoife. 'Oh, I …' The page shook in his hand and his foot tapped violently. Aoife only then seemed to realise her error, so caught up was she in her fun prank. Before he embarrassed both of us, I took a quick sweep around the group to check their poems.

'Adam,' I said, 'they're all terrible, easily worse than yours, especially Fintan's. Yours is good enough.'

Adam looked at his page.

'Honestly, if you read this, people will like it. Aoife will like it.'

He cleared his throat and began. 'This … this poem is called "Tuesday Night in Turner's Cross":

The footballer fell over another.
The floodlights crackled and spat.
I saw the linesman check his watch.
No worries, as the watcher dipped his chips in the red …

'Sorry, that's as far as I got.'

The circle clapped and Adam sat down as quickly as possible.

'Very interesting, Adam. It was evocative,' Niamh said.

Adam, that sneak! That sounded way better out loud. I hoped he realised that this kind of squalid poetry was the result of not consulting me.

'Who will read next? Oh, Fintan?'

As Fintan recited his really detailed ode to his ex-girlfriend (turns out there aren't many words that rhyme with Nicola), Aoife wrote a note and passed it to Adam.

I'm so so so so sorry. :(

After a few moments, Adam wrote underneath it and slid it back to her.

You're sorry now? Wait till you hear my other poems!

She took the page and sighed with relief.

Don't threaten me, buddy. You haven't heard my masterpiece yet.

The sound of clapping interrupted the paper exchange.

'Fintan, that was … informative. Who's next? Okay, Aoife, go ahead.'

I noticed he hadn't thanked me for my help.

TWENTY-TWO

My exact nature remained something of a mystery to both me and Adam. After some research (this research being *Paranormal Activity* movies and a documentary on YouTube with some guy from *Star Trek*), we felt that if I wasn't a figment of Adam's imagination, I was most likely a ghost, but where did that place me in a theological context? Was I an occurrence of a previously unknown force of the universe, or was I a messenger from Heaven or Hell? I know I am not from purgatory, as that's on Earth – I have visited and it's an afternoon all-ages gig in The Loft.

Before continuing, I will take a moment to describe The Loft. It looked like something out of the nightmares of an alcoholic. The clientele were sullen kids Adam's age and middle-aged men with long beards, gentlemen whose presence at an all-ages gig would be of concern, except there is no evidence they have left their stools since the heyday of heavy metal, a period which can only be placed definitively as 'Before your time, kid' or 'Back in the day'.

This awfulness wasn't helped when the only person who could communicate with me was busy staring at his hand. A symbol had been scrawled on it in pen by a girl with multiple piercings at the front entrance in the unlikely event that he would want to return after leaving. (One advantage of being a ghost is that you don't have to pay for gigs, especially ones that look like they are going to be crappy.)

'I think mine is a hashtag,' said Aoife, who then grabbed Adam's hand to more closely observe his – an a with a circle around it. 'I think you're an at.'

'An ant?' said Adam, making no effort to pull his hand back after Aoife rudely stole it from him.

'No, the symbol at! Like for emails.'

'Ah, I can see it now.'

When Linda returned Aoife finally released her grasp and Adam took back his hand.

'If you need to pee, I really recommend hanging on till you get home. It's a sewage pipe in there. When are Douglas and Barry on?' asked Linda, readjusting her dashing hat.

'I think they're on second,' said Aoife.

They were on third. First up were Defenestrated Cattle, a four-piece band with two drummers and no singers. I'm not sure what they were going for but they didn't achieve it. Second was Cannibal Cannonball. Or possibly Cannonball Cannibal. The lead singer mumbled a bit over some screeching guitars and a laptop played clips from a war film. Finally, after their cover of 'Hallelujah' (key comment from the stools: 'Bet those kids haven't even heard the Jeff Buckley original'), Douglas, Barry and their new bassist Sinead walked onto the stage, all dressed in capes made of tinfoil.

Douglas grabbed the microphone and screamed, 'EVERY-ONE, PREPARE TO HAVE YOUR EARDRUMS MOISTENED BY THE MUSICAL STYLINGS OF …

THE LAYPERSONS!'

'Douglas, give us a second. I can't find my drumsticks,' said Barry, searching his pockets.

'Don't worry. I'll stall. Ahem ... audience, while the band gets ready, I shall read to you from The Laypersons' manifesto. Number 1: we reject all notions of melody. Number 2: we embrace the cacophony of the everyday. Number 3–'

'Found them!' said Barry. He remembered he had tucked them into his shoe.

'MUSIC TIME!'

So they began. It was loud and weird and difficult to follow. It sounded incorrect at every turn, a series of intentional missteps. Also the capes kept making crinkling noises that the microphones picked up. However, to my surprise, I quite liked it.

I looked over to see what Adam thought, but he was distracted by Aoife whispering in his ear. Whatever she said, he smiled. I looked at Linda, who was waving her arms around intensely. After a bass solo, the song abruptly stopped.

'EVERYONE!' shouted Douglas. 'THAT WAS OUR FIRST AND LAST SONG! WE ONLY HAVE ONE, THAT'S WHY IT'S SEVENTEEN MINUTES LONG.'

The crowd clapped.

'NOW, DON'T BE ASSHOLES AND PLEASE WAIT FOR THE NEXT BAND! WE WERE THE LAYPERSONS!'

This led to more clapping and one 'hell, yeah' from a guy in the corner, who was apparently very excited. It would seem a lot of people were here to see the next band, The Daughters Dreadnaught, as a crowd quickly formed at the front of the stage. Not wishing to be seen as assholes, the gang hung on for them and even moved in closer to the throng of sweaty teens, some of whom seemed to have lost their shirts.

There was a quick tap on Aoife's shoulder.

'Excuse me, I came to see this band,' said its owner, a random skinny dude.

'And?' said Aoife.

'Could you move your head? I can't see the stage,' he said.

Aoife exhaled a little. 'Dude, there is literally loads of space.'

'I don't see why I should move. I was here first.'

'Buddy, there's no need to be a dick,' said Linda, joining her friend.

'How am I being a dick? It's not my fault her hair is in the way.'

'I am actually a person,' said Aoife, whose patience was being exhausted.

Adam so far had added nothing to this little scene. I could see him standing there uncomfortably, squirming with indecision. The dude, however, was firm in his decision to be difficult.

'I'm just saying, in this country …'

'If you are about to suggest that I belong to a different country other than the one I'm currently standing in–'

'Why are you making this a race thing? I just want to–'

'Stand over there instead? That's a great idea,' said Aoife. The guy looked like he was about to say something else but then gave up. He walked away, muttering something under his breath about that not looking like an Irish tan to him, and stood at the other side of the room, choosing to express his indignation by glaring at her instead of the stage.

Victorious from their set, Douglas, Barry and Sinead rejoined the group. 'Aw, I knew we were bad,' said Barry, seeing their faces.

'No, sorry. You were great,' said Linda, 'it's just that guy over there was being a jerk. Aoife embarrassed him though. It was pretty epic.'

Adam said nothing. His face was as red as a berry.

'Excellent,' said Douglas. 'Does anyone wish to celebrate the vanquishing of this cretin by helping us load the amps into my mother's car?'

The rest nodded and, as they walked, Adam found himself at the back of the group with Aoife.

'Aoife?' he said timidly.

'Hm?' said Aoife, dragging herself back from a faraway place, where I like to imagine she was visiting a thousand cruel punishments on that dude.

'Sorry I didn't do anything there.'

'Oh? That's okay. Well, not really, but it's not your fault. There are a lot of assholes in the world.'

'If it happens again, I promise I'll be more effective back-up.'

'Don't worry,' said Aoife, with a tight smile, 'it will happen again.'

TWENTY-THREE

I wasn't born yesterday (at this point, I was almost half a year old) and I could see what was happening, though I ignored it for as long as possible. Perhaps I was even in denial, but the truth was plain when I saw him gaze openly at his laptop. On Facebook there was a photograph from the gig, just the two of them, together. Tagged. Adam and Aoife looking at each other's hands. Laughing, and not the usual kind of laughing together, the kind of laughing I saw that first night I explored the city in all its heat and pairings of bodies on window sills.

'I sincerely hope you aren't getting any ideas,' I said.

'What do you mean?' he said.

'That photo!' I said.

'So? It's me and Aoife. People can hang out if they so please.'

'You don't want to be starting any hanky panky.'

Adam considered the photo.

'Do you think she and I—'

'No!'

'What does it matter to you anyway?'

I had felt in recent weeks rather neglected and I didn't like it. Granted, I didn't want to say this out loud, so instead I said, 'Look, sometimes you have to trust your gut, and my gut says this is a bad idea.'

'I would heed this advice, except you don't have a gut.'

Adam looked back at the photo, really looked at it and finally 'Liked' it. He wrote underneath it, *Crazy gig, huh?*

'I'm merely concerned for your mental health.'

'Thanks, pal,' he said, giving me a thumbs up, which I believe was sarcastic. The cheek!

A moment later, she liked his comment. At which he smiled.

'That doesn't mean anything,' I warned. 'From what I've seen, people will like anything.'

It would only be a matter of time before he'd be foolish and decide to make a move.

'You know, I might ask her if she wants to do something together,' he said about ten seconds later, waiting for my approval, which he was not going to receive.

'That's a terrible idea. She'll say no and you'll be embarrassed. Then the two of you won't be comfortable hanging out and you'll have to leave the group. No one will want to be your friend any more.'

Adam wasn't listening. More of the neglect I was talking about!

Instead of heeding my advice, he bounced off his bed and strolled out the door. He sent a text asking who was around and, wouldn't ya know it, Aoife was about. He walked to town in a heedless stride, his head full of ideas. He found her sitting outside O'Briens with a near empty bottle of Coke. He waved but she didn't notice him. He walked up to her, but with a less confident step. With any luck, his fear would stop this.

'Aoife?'

'No response. I'd say abandon this,' I said.

Nervously, he tapped her on the shoulder. She turned with some surprise, smiled and took off her headphones.

'Oh, hey, Adam!' she said with a wave, even though he was literally centimetres away from her.

'Oh, hi. I … Can I ask you something?'

'Bail. Bail. Bail,' I said.

'Sure.'

He brushed his hair away from his forehead.

'Oi! Harry!' said a fellow passing by.

After the hospital, he had grown his fringe out in an attempt to hide his self-inflicted scar. Unfortunately this had the inexplicable side effect of random people calling him 'Harry'. Perhaps he looked like a friend of theirs.

'Ah … what are you listening to?' Adam said, already red with embarrassment.

'Have a listen.'

Adam put the headphones on and I hovered closer so I could hear it too. As you may have guessed, I don't like being left out of things. Aoife pressed play and the headphones filled with several layers of unlistenable static and noise. It was so loud I could hear it. From Adam's face, I could tell it was hurting his eardrums. Not for the first time I was glad I lacked physical eardrums to rupture.

'Pretty good, right?' said Aoife with perplexing enthusiasm. 'It's by Djevelen Katt. They're are a Norwegian Death Metal band. Their lead singer died in a sword fight with the bassist. It was all over the Internet for a while there. Hang on, I'll play something else.'

Aoife watched expectantly as Adam struggled with the music. He didn't want to disappoint her, so he pretended it was in some way listenable, which was a mistake, as this only encouraged her and she decided to play him something else. The music switched to a slightly more melodic piece, where the dense noises were interrupted every so often by the sound of a man screaming.

'That's Skumle Sko. You can tell it's one of their later ones since it's a bit more pop-y.'

Adam signalled for the next one. The music now changed to a cacophonous crash of notes and fragments of a woman singing.

'WHO'S THIS?'

'It's …' Aoife checked her screen, 'a Katy Perry track. Linda gave it to me but the file got corrupted by my computer, but I liked it this way so I kept it.'

Adam pulled off the headphones. 'That was … something.'

'Did you like it?'

'If you go out with her, you'll have to pretend to like this music all the time,' I said.

'Yeah, no, not really.'

'*SIGH!* Not everyone can have as great taste in music as me,' she said. Blast, why couldn't she have been offended?

'Heh heh, this is true. Would you …'

This follow-up was mercifully interrupted by Douglas, who stormed towards them. He had a fury in his eyes, as if he'd had to listen to Aoife's playlist for more than twenty minutes.

Douglas had a flare for entrances. Even in broad daylight he was capable of sudden appearances, as if teleported from a far-off planet made of angst. He pointed at them. 'You two, have you seen that traitor?'

'Hey, Douglas,' said the two in unison. 'Who?'

'Who? Barry, of course. We have a gig next week and he has pulled out, with some feeble excuse. I'm broadcasting it now! Barry Lynch is out of The Spoken Mystics!'

'The who?'

'We decided to go in a new direction after our first gig. The time was right, at least it was before he abandoned me. Now, it's just me and Sinead, and we have nothing to talk about. She's always on about PlayStation games. She knows I'm from an Xbox family. It's impossible to deal with her.'

'Why can't he play?' said Adam.

'Oh, something stupid. His sister is getting married or something. Can either of you drum?'

'No. My dad has a drum machine if that helps,' said Adam. 'He was in a Blur tribute band when he was younger.'

'I don't know what a blur is, but it will have to do. Alas, I knew technology would overtake the human element of the band, I just never dreamed … Well, we'll have to rename the band again,' said Douglas as he wandered away.

This distraction gone, Adam tried again.

'Anyway I was thinking–'

'Hi,' said a familiar black and red jumper. *Beep beep.* Barry checked his phone and his face became terse.

'Did you tell Douglas to replace me with a drum machine?'

Adam was beginning to sweat. 'Well ... Congratulations to your sister.'

'Eh, what about her?'

'She's getting married?'

'That'd be weird. She's about eight years old.'

'Aren't you going to her wedding on Saturday?'

'Oh! No, I just told Douglas that because I have to play in my cousin's band on Saturday. I didn't want to but she's blackmailing me.'

'How?'

'She saw me clean up some paint with the good towels and bin them after.'

'Busted.'

'Busted indeed. You charlatan!' shouted Douglas, who jumped out from seemingly nowhere. 'Not only do you betray me by joining a different band, but you lie to me about your sister getting married. The most sacred vow between two people!'

'In my defence, you did meet her. You knew she was way younger than me!'

'Barry, it has been a while since I last saw her and time makes fools of us all. Besides your word means nothing. It's too late. Adam has already promised me a robotic replacement.'

'Wait, I still have to ask my dad if you can use it,' said Adam.

'And I'm far superior to a drum machine.'

'We shall see. Adam, bring us to your house and I'll judge if Barry is truly the equal of this mechanised musician.'

'What's going on?' said Linda, just joining us.

'We are all going to Adam's house.'

'Cool! I've never seen it.'

'Wait, I … Sure. I just need to check if it's okay.'

Adam was looking stressed as he rang his mother. 'Hey, Mum. Would it be okay if I brought some friends home with me in a few minutes?'

'Great! Do! I'd love to meet them,' she said.

'She's okay about it, but only for a little bit,' he said to everyone after hanging up the phone.

***

'I like the gnome,' said Linda.

'Oh yeah, that's my dad's. He thinks they're funny. Ha!' said Adam.

I wondered what he was so nervous about. Was it his friends meeting his family or his family meeting his friends? He opened the door and, despite what he may have hoped, his mother was there immediately.

'Hello, Mrs Murphy!' said everyone in a sweet chorus.

'Hello! You must be Adam's friends.'

'You have a cool house,' said Barry, admiring a tacky-looking vase.

'Oh, well, you have a cool jumper.'

Barry beamed, vindicated in his decision to wear the same thing day in, day out. Everyone else rolled their eyes. After Adam introduced them all, they travelled up to his room, where Adam's dad was directed to bring his drum machine.

'Your room is a bit sparse,' said Linda. 'You should get a rug or something.'

'I like it,' said Aoife. 'Very modern.'

'Oh, yeah,' said Adam.

'There you go, lads,' said Dad, bearing an electronic gift. Douglas brushed off the thin layer of dust and pressed one of the buttons. It created a steady beat.

'Well, it's already surpassed your shoddy timekeeping, Barry.'

'Enjoy!' said Dad, who stopped a moment before leaving to stealthily point at Aoife with a questioning face. Adam cringed hard. This was actually quite amusing.

'Oh, I love this book,' said Aoife, pointing at one of the ones he hadn't read all of.

Adam was relieved she hadn't seen his father's not too subtle communication. 'Oh, that one, me too.'

'My favourite bit is the moment with the test.'

'Me too. Man, it's been so long since I read it.'

Adam was an inexpert liar. It was a bit embarrassing to watch really. You could almost hear his heartbeat speed up.

'Oh, I can increase the tempo too!' said Douglas, playing

with the drum machine. 'Wow, Barry, you have been rendered obsolete by the latest technology of the nineties.'

'This is total BS.'

'Shoot, I have to go,' said Linda, noticing the time. 'My mother is making me go shopping for "sensible shoes".'

'Me too. I need to practise with my new band member, Barry 1,' said Douglas, hugging the drum machine and leaving the room.

'Shouldn't it be Barry 2?' said Barry following him out to the hall.

'It's really more of a ranking.'

It was just Aoife and Adam (and me) in the room now. I willed Adam not to say anything. She smiled at him and he smiled back. His eyes looked around frantically for something to delay her.

'Adam! Can you help your father in the garden? No worries if your friends are still here.'

'Duty calls. I'll see ya later,' said Aoife.

'Yeah, I'll get on to you about that.'

'About what?'

'Later?'

'Bye.' She waved goodbye, a FRIENDS ONLY wave, I hoped, since their romance was something that was never going to happen.

He showed her to the door. After she popped her headphones back on and walked out the gate, he joined his father in the garden, who handed him a trowel.

'Is it okay if Douglas borrows the drum machine?'

'Well, since I saw him walk out the door with it already, I guess it had better be.'

'Thanks.'

Adam began to dig.

'She's pretty,' Dad said. Adam once again blushed.

***

Hey, want to see a movie?

Aoife, You, me, movie?

Yo, we should all meet next week, except maybe just you and me?

Like a lovesick fool, Adam was typing text messages that would never be sent. He kept writing them and hovering his thumb over the send button, but in the end, he deleted each one. His cowardice was quite amusing, I must say. He started again.

I LIKE YOU! WE SHOULD GO SEE A MOVIE AND MAYBE KISS!

'Sure you want to send that?'

'Yes! No! I don't know!'

He tossed the phone away. It landed on his bed with a soft thud. 'I'd better not. I guess I don't really know her and I'm only just making friends with that whole group.'

'That's true. Don't want to make things weird.'

Adam took some deep breaths. It was settled for now.

Beep beep.

His eyes widened and he raced to the bed. It was a message from Aoife. He had accidentally sent the last text. The impact with the bed must have been hard enough to activate the send button on his touchscreen. He closed his eyes and picked up the phone.

> That's a great idea. The first one that is, we'll see about the second part. ;) Want to see something tomorrow?

I kid you not, Adam did a little dance. He was very, very excited, so excited that he briefly forgot to answer back.

> Yes

Beep beep.

> That was some straight talking partner.
> I assume from the briefness of your reply
> that I will select the movie we see.

Sure.

Well I can see I shall be the more verbose on
this date. So I insist you pick a time and
place. Otherwise I will have DONE ALL THE
WORK HERE which is not terribly romantic.

Adam grinned to himself.

Maybe it's romantic for me …

Oh God, this was horrifying. *Beep beep.*

Ah a victory for feminism! :P I notice that
you still haven't stated a preferred time or place.

7ish? At the Omniplex?

Excellent. Mr Murphy I shall meet you at
The Pictuirlann at 6. :)

LOL

I would like to point out that at this moment Adam did not
laugh out loud. He barely made a sound, simply smiling like a
fool. Love makes liars out of us all apparently.

Beep beep.

I'm fairly confident that is the first time you
ever wrote LOL. I'm touched. See you then!

See you then!

He stared at the phone a little longer. 'I should leave it there, right? No more messages?'

'Yes! You said, "See you then."'

'I could have phrased it better …'

'Go to bed.'

Adam went to bed and was too excited to sleep. Since he wasn't in snoozeville, I wasn't able to go for a walk. Instead I got to hang out and listen to him blab about Aoife.

I didn't know why he was so excited. He still had to go on the date and maybe then she would realise that she didn't like him. It could still all go wrong. This hadn't occurred to him, so I suggested it in the hope he would calm down enough to fall asleep, but then he became too worried to fall asleep. This was not the desired effect but it was preferable to Happy, Happy, Joy, Joy.

TWENTY-FOUR

On their first date, Aoife lied. Instead of a cinema, she led him to a grey brick with a door.

'What's this?' Adam said.

'A cinema. Look at the sign.'

Written in faded red were the words 'Pictiurlann Cinema'.

'I come here to watch weird films. They show loads, especially horror ones.'

Underneath the sign was a cracked glass box, trapping a poster which featured a woman holding a typewriter while standing in the sea. She looked unhappy.

We walked in and there was a bearded gentleman sitting behind the desk, reading a book with no picture on the cover. He looked up and recognised Aoife. As they chatted in what turned out to be a surprisingly lengthy discussion about something that had been showing last week, Adam read the programme of upcoming movies on the wall. None of the names were familiar and many seemed to involve pale, black-haired women staring.

'Hey, Adam, do you want a drink?'

'Ah, Club Orange?'

'That and I'll have a cup of tea.'

The bearded fellow handed them the tickets and their drinks.

'Oh, which screen?' said Adam.

'Only the one,' he said, pointing at a door where a cool woman wearing a floppy hat was standing. She ripped their tickets in half and sent them in.

I followed the couple into screen one (and only). We were the only ones there, save for a second bearded man in the back row. We sat and watched the film, Aoife and Adam together and me several seats back, because Adam kept glaring at me when I sat next to him. The film was strange and I'm not sure I liked it. Mostly the characters kept having loud arguments in French about a book.

I think the two of them were getting bored, too, as Aoife began whispering into Adam's ear.

About midway through the film, the French woman has taken her Czech lover's collection of books and begun to drop them in a river. The man runs up to her and grabs her wrist. The woman smiles for a moment and with her free hand, grabs his cheek, dragging it down to her face. She bites it and they proceed to press things together on the river bank, underneath a tree and then suddenly in a rotting cottage.

I looked back at the couple and saw them giggling. Aoife made an exaggerated yawning gesture and landed her arm on the back of Adam's neck. They looked at each other and laughed out loud. They were shushed by the one other film-goer.

After the film they had a meal, at least as close to a meal as two teenagers with limited funds could afford: two burgers in Hamburger Inn. He had a chicken burger and she had a quarter-pounder with cheese. They shared chips.

'So what did you think of the movie?' said Adam.

'Oh, it was very intellectual, so I enjoyed it as I'm very clever. If you didn't like it, I understand. Those films aren't for everyone,' said Aoife, mock solemnly.

'Oh, I really liked it. I really enjoyed how it was about … feelings and things. It really made me think … about things and, eh, feelings.'

They stared at each other, with fixed solemn expressions.

'Gosh, aren't we very smart?'

She couldn't continue, as uncontrollable giggles had taken over. Adam joined in with his own giggles, which when combined mutated into out and out laughter. Unimpressed, their table neighbour glared, but they didn't notice.

'No, it was pretty rubbish,' said Aoife.

'I hadn't a clue what was going on. To be honest, I was hoping for dinosaurs.'

'Dinosaurs would have been good. French ones.'

'They could wear stripy jumpers.'

'Ride bicycles!'

'Carry baguettes with their tiny arms!'

'Excuse me,' said the man sitting next to them, 'I'm trying to eat my meal in peace!' They both said sorry, and continued eating their burgers in silence until Adam stopped and took a breath.

'Aoife?'

'Yes?'

'Je suis un grand T-Rex!'

They both burst out laughing.

To finish the evening, they took a walk along the river towards the Lee Fields. The sky was dark. Their conversation had begun to become embarrassingly sincere. They discussed many things, like their houses, school and other inane subjects. They started to talk about our writing.

'I liked your new story,' said Aoife, 'the one with the trees. It's a bit creepy. My kind of thing.'

'Thank you. I'm glad you liked it. I'm only starting to properly write things down. But I'm enjoying it.'

'Oh, I've written stories for years. I've piles of them at home.'

'Why did you start writing?' Adam said.

'I read a lot so it seemed like the right thing to do. You?' Aoife said.

'Ah, I don't read that much. I just kind of like writing. It makes me feel ... in control of things.'

Aoife took a moment, glanced along the water. 'Actually I do have another reason for writing. Have you ever noticed that books have a default?'

'Um ...'

'Sorry. You know if you are reading a book and the lead character's appearance isn't described in detail that, you know, they could be anyone from anywhere. Like, no one specifically says that Matilda isn't Chinese.'

'Right.'

'But she's not Chinese. We assume she is not, because

we have a default in our head. Unless it's said otherwise, we assume she is a white English kid because she probably is a white English kid. And it's the same in loads of books. We can pretend they aren't necessarily one thing, but we know that they are because there is no reason to think they are not.'

'I guess,' Adam said.

'So when I write a story, I know it's me because I wrote it.'

'But you write about spaceships, wizards, vampires and things.'

'That's because I want to meet vampires and go on spaceships and things.'

Adam walked along some more without saying anything, considering what Aoife had said. 'I kinda see what you mean.'

'I'm just saying I don't want to be hidden in my own books. So even if I don't say it, I know it's me! I want to do all the things – romance, adventure, horror, you know … stuff!'

'Well, maybe I can help you with the first one of those,' said Adam.

Aoife laughed. 'Mr Murphy, that was a bold segue.'

'It was,' he said, surprised by his own charm. He wasn't the only one.

Adam and Aoife drew in closer. The light of the street lamp above them illuminated their faces, as he pushed the hair from her cheek. They pressed their faces together. This seemed to last a long time and, once they kissed, it seemed to release a dam of pent-up smooching as they pressed their mouths together repeatedly.

Eventually they stopped and began walking back towards town, dopily holding hands, refusing to break apart even when it was necessary and interrupting their walk many times to kiss again, expanding a twenty-minute walk to nearly an hour. They laughed and invented jokes and were generally being cute. It was nauseating. If I had a stomach, it would have been turning.

Their final kiss of the night was when she grabbed her bus home, her standing on the bus reaching down for one last memento. The bus left and they waved goodbye to each other as if it would be the last time they would ever see each other. Adam walked away from the bus stop and a few moments later there was a beep from his pocket. He checked it, smiled and responded immediately.

'Ahem,' I said, clearing my nonexistent throat.

'Oh, yeah. Heh, I completely forgot you were there.'

I'd noticed.

'How do you think the date went? Oh wait, I got a message. Give me a second.'

I said nothing but this didn't bother him. It bothered me, though.

TWENTY-FIVE

A few days later, Aoife was waiting at the school gates for him. I felt this was an early warning sign of clinginess and told Adam as much.

'Stop being weird,' he said.

'Well, maybe you should stop talking to yourself,' I said.

He ignored me. As we approached, she put on a mock impressed expression.

'You, sir, go to a fancy school,' she said teasingly.

'It's not that ... well, of course, here at St Jude's we produce a higher class of boy, future leaders some may say,' Adam said. 'I didn't expect to see you here.'

'We finished early today because ... actually, I don't know the reason. Someone was visiting, I think. Anyway, I thought I'd ogle your handsome schoolmates.'

'Oh really? Is the ogling good so far?'

'Not great, but it did improve considerably a moment ago.'

'I'm sure it did.'

They kissed and I realised this would probably become a regular thing. Yay.

I noticed that as the other students passed there was a general look of approval. Clearly Adam having a girlfriend was a positive development in their eyes.

In an effort to enjoy the flouting of their new social arrangement, the couple walked into town, holding hands like two otters in a pond. (Aoife had sent Adam a YouTube video of this earlier in the week. It was, admittedly, adorable.) Their hands were so tightly clasped together that it took a second too long to separate when they entered a favoured café. Linda spotted it and Aoife spotted Linda spotting it.

'Ah … his hand was cold. Very poor circulation,' said Aoife.

'It's true. I should buy gloves immediately,' affirmed Adam. Linda shook her head.

'Really? Aoife? Adam? I find that hard to believe. Not because I know for sure whether or not our friend here has a circulation problem, but I do notice flushed cheeks, coy smiles, little glances – all classic signs of hanky panky. Canoodling. Pitching woo.'

'Canoodling!' shouted Douglas, who was waiting at the counter for his food. 'What romantic entanglement am I not privy to?'

'Aoife and Adam! They've been kissing!' Linda shouted.

'My word! That is news!' Douglas shouted.

'AHEM,' said the man behind the counter, pointing at a sign that read 'No Shouting'.

'Oh, you've got a sign and everything for it now,' said Douglas. 'That should really cut down on those loud scallywags.'

The man sighed loudly and handed him his sandwich.

They all convened together. 'I'm not going to lie. I'm not surprised at this news. I'm not happy, but this is entirely due to my rejection of any sentimental romance. So I won't give you my blessing, but I will also not object to it.'

'That's as good as it gets,' said Linda. 'Hey, did you get me chips?'

'Get your own chips.'

'You know they won't sell them on their own, only as a side. They even made a sign for it.'

'They have really gotten into making signs recently, and not fun ones like the orange making friends with the ice cream,' said Aoife.

'Balls. I'll have to wait till I get home. Oh, that reminds me, I'm having a birthday party next weekend.'

'Who's invited?'

'Me, you three, Barry.'

Douglas gave a very audible sniff. I took it that Douglas and Barry had not mended fences.

'That's it. Oh, and maybe Sinead,' said Linda.

'I'm avoiding Sinead,' said Douglas. 'Since the addition of the drum machine, she wants to push The Spoken Mystics in more of an electronic direction. I refuse to, naturally, as I don't have an electro haircut.'

'Oh, and since it's only a few days before Halloween, it's a costume party! And as it's my birthday you can't not dress up.'

'Did you ever have concerns about the fact you're born so close to our most pagan of holidays?' said Douglas.

'I haven't. Although it would explain my mysterious floating over my bed.'

Everything was just getting worse and worse. From then on, Adam and Aoife would become 'Adam & Aoife'. Frankly I found it rather insidious. Two people becoming one unit, this inseparable union of opinions and thoughts. I'm only able to communicate with one person, so I didn't want to only speak to half of one.

GHOST SICKNESS

by Adam Murphy

All night, every night I heard that damned whistle. It was a dry, long tune that may have once been merry, but has since been drained entirely of happiness. It haunted me. I couldn't stop it, I couldn't escape it. It came from beneath the bed which had served as my prison for so long.

It was a wintery May. My forehead burned hot and my feet ran cold. I was very ill this time, not the worst spell I had encountered but very bad indeed. I'm habitually sick, almost an unwanted hobby that my body insists on indulging. I spend most of my year under these stiff sheets, only occasionally strong enough to venture outside onto the balcony.

'You'll be okay, Tom. You have nothing to worry about,' my wife said. When I am ill, my beloved Harmony was usually my caretaker. Our relationship started like that. She was my nurse and, out of either affection or pity, she fell in love with me. We married and now she makes sure that I eat my food, take my pills.

Last week, I asked her if she could hear the whistle.

'What whistle?' she said. I could see she had no idea what I was saying.

'Nothing. It must be a bird,' I said. I did not feel the need to worry her unnecessarily.

'There are sparrows a lot this time of year. Do they whistle?'

'I don't know. I guess they must.' Thus the whistle remained my terrible secret, a ghost noise that eluded all but me.

As she carried out her tasks, it taunted me, drove me mad. I needed to know what it was. An enemy? My dear beloved gas-lighting me? No, I was being paranoid. It was probably something as simple as wind passing through some obscure route from the pipes below the floorboards. It was an old house, perfectly suitable for haunting by malignant spirits.

When she left and I attempted to sleep, the whistling continued. To distract myself, I grabbed a dusty book of interesting facts and I read them out. 'This is something interesting,' I said to the air. 'Did you know that when members of Native American tribes became ill, some blamed their malady on the presence of a deceased enemy or relative, a spirit trying to ruin them or take them to the afterlife?'

In response, the whistle persisted, but this time it played an old cowboy tune I recognised from a western I had seen as a child. This was a new development.

'Are you such a dreadful apparition? Are you my deceased aunt who died at sea one Christmas morning?'

The whistle changed to a sea shanty. 'What shall we do with a drunken sailor?' it asked. Clearly it was mocking me now.

I lay there as it blew jaunty sailor songs over and over. When I heard the grandfather clock in the hall strike 12 midnight, I decided that enough was enough. With a mighty heave, I pushed myself off the bed and onto the floor in a heap of blankets and bones. The whistle made a winding down noise, which finished with a bum note. Once I recovered my breath, I looked underneath my *bed but all I could see was a dark chasm, a contained void that was deep and infinite.*

'Show yourself!' I said. Instead it whistled a taunting tune, which I recognised but could not place. With my hand I opened a drawer in my nightstand. Groping, I found what I was looking for, a book of matches. I lit one of the two remaining sticks but it illuminated nothing. I flicked it in but it was swallowed by the sheer darkness.

The whistling was louder and faster. It was driving me mad. I needed some relief. I needed to see what was making that bloody noise.

I pulled out a page from a book that was resting on the nightstand. Using my one remaining matchstick, I set it alight. Holding it up like a makeshift torch, I pushed it in underneath. Still nothing.

I could smell burning fabric. The sheets! I'd set the bed on fire. I attempted to pull out my hand but something grabbed it!

'Let go, you monster!' I shouted. But it held my arm in place. I couldn't see it but I could feel its cold hand, its long nails digging into my flesh. The flame was scorching the bed above it. Soon the whole bed was alight and the flames could not be stopped. My blankets, my pillows, my sheets disintegrating before my eyes.

Before I got burned, the hand finally let go, and with my remaining strength I rolled away out of danger. Finally I could see them, lit by the fire – a pair of familiar eyes.

Harmony reappeared in shock. Using a heavy blanket from the cupboard, she doused the flames, but it was too late, the whole thing was destroyed. She looked at me with confusion and I had no explanation for her.

Well, I won. The whistling stopped, but now I have nowhere to sleep.

TWENTY-SIX

'Is that true, the bit about Native Americans?' asked Dr Moore.

'Yip, at least it says so on the Internet.'

'Well, you can always trust the Internet.'

'It's called ghost sickness.'

'Oh, of course, that's the name of the story. Well, I liked it, it was very insightful. A little dark.'

As an exercise, Dr Moore had asked Adam to show him one of his short stories. So, feeling inspired, he decided to write one specially for the session. I enjoyed working on it, although Adam was a bit more in control of our dynamic than usual, often dismissing my contributions with an 'I'm not sure that works' or a 'That's good, but it might work better if …'

'They generally are,' said Adam, leaning back in his chair. He had become significantly more relaxed over these visits; in the beginning he'd perched on the edge of the chair, rigid with tension.

'The supernatural figure in it is interesting,' said Dr Moore.

'Is it?'

'Is it?' I echoed.

'My college minor is English lit, so you'll have to indulge some academic reading.'

Adam squirmed a little and looked at me for a second. It seemed like a 'conversation' was about to happen.

'The villain is a mysterious figure that only your main character can see and hear. It's pretty clear.'

'Is it?' repeated Adam.

Actually, that did sound familiar. I wondered if the good doctor had figured out what was going on with Adam. After all these weeks had he finally worked out that I was here, following Adam's every step?

'Clearly this monster is a metaphor for the protagonist's mental illness, the awful nagging thoughts that make him ill, attacking him when he is low.'

'It is?' said Adam. 'But it's clearly a physical thing. He's ill.'

'Oh yes, as a metaphor. Often people with mental health issues describe them as physical ailments and they often manifest as such. For example, headaches, sleeping problems, lack of appetite. The brain and body are quite interlinked, you know. Why did you mention familiar eyes at the end?'

'I thought it sounded creepy.'

'Are you sure that was all? A man confined to his bed for reasons beyond his control, who sees very few people. It sounds like the character was seeing himself ... and he didn't like it.'

This was a surprise. Questions flooded my mind. Had Adam tricked me? Writing a short story about how much he hates me under my nose? I felt a strange anger rise inside me. Is this what I was to him? A strange whistle under a bed? How pathetic. If he is writing me into stories, I should look like him, except a brooding, handsome version, maybe with black eyes, like a dark double in a movie that the hero must defeat. But no, I'm a pair of eyes and a disembodied hand that makes whistling noises.

'I don't think it's about anything, it's just a silly horror story,' he said.

Too late, Adam, I already know what you think.

'If you say so. One last thing, though: I think it's significant how you end it.'

'Uh …'

'Your character burns the bed, symbolically destroying the life he is confined to, although to his possible detriment.'

The bell rang. Time was up.

'I'll just finish my thought. It's possible this story suggests that you are afraid to get better and leave your bed, as it were, for fear that you will destroy everything–'

'But–'

'… or else you are afraid that you are going to make a rash decision that you feel is out of your control. It's something to think about.'

'See you next week.'

'See you next week, Adam.'

We stepped out of the office and I noticed that Adam was scrutinising me.

'I can't believe you wrote a story about me and made me some kind of monster that is ruining your life,' I said.

'Hang on, that was just his take on it.'

'Who kept you company all those months before you got your new "friends"?'

'You have literally no choice. And anyway, no one else can see you, so if you didn't talk to me, you'd have no one,' he replied.

'Which apparently makes me some fictional demon!'

'Well, to be fair, I don't know if you are real or just a figment of my imagination.'

'Of course I'm real. I saw Chris before he killed himself, and you didn't see that,' I said. I was more defensive than I liked here.

Adam thought about this. 'No, you told me you saw a handsome boy in a well-fitting school uniform. It wasn't until after you saw the picture of Chris that you identified who you saw. That's awfully vague. If you are part of my imagination, then I could easily have applied that identification to what you saw.'

Adam appeared lost in thought as we walked on. I could think of nothing to say. We passed a man standing at a bus stop, reading something off an electronic device.

'Tell ya what,' he said, 'if you go behind that guy and can tell me what he is reading, then I will believe you are a real ghost.'

That would have been the simple solution, but the suggestion that it was necessary to demonstrate my existence was infuriating to me and I said as much. Loudly. Repeatedly.

'Okay, okay. Calm down. It was only a thought.'

'I'm only a thought, you mean.'

He walked faster and faster, as if he could get rid of me

(which he can't) and he looked at me cock-eyed for much of the trip home. On the way we stopped at the shop, the small one near his house.

'Hi,' said the bored girl at the counter.

Adam passed her with a wave. He grabbed some milk and bread that his mother had told him to pick up on his way home.

We joined the back of the queue in silence. I was feeling many emotions – anger, confusion, fear, betrayal. Perhaps I needed my own therapist.

'Why don't you tell him about me since you hate me so much? If you think I'm a figment of your imagination, couldn't you just talk me away?'

'I don't want to look like a complete weirdo,' he wrote on his phone screen, so I could read it. (This was a new technique for communication in public spaces that we had invented to avoid the appearance of Adam talking to himself.)

'But if you don't want me around, wouldn't it be worth it?'

'This is ridiculous.'

'It's the principle! You want to get rid of me.'

'Don't you want to go?'

At that moment I wanted it more than anything, but I wanted to be the one doing the leaving, not the one being dumped. Anyway, this whole conversation had got me confused and doubting myself.

Before I could answer he wrote, 'Since you think it's such a good idea, I'll ring him now and tell him all about you.'

He opened his contacts and found Dr Moore's number. His hovering thumb put the panic in me. I didn't want him to do anything hasty.

'You can get rid of me but then that'd be it for the writing. You've only been able to write stories since I arrived. I disappear, the stories do too. You think your precious girlfriend will want to hang out with you then?'

Adam considered that.

'That's €4.' The bored girl sounded irritated, as if this wasn't the first time she had said this.

'Oh, yeah, sorry.'

He pulled the change from his pocket and handed it to her. Then he put the phone back in his pocket. It may sound petty, but this victory made me feel wanted and valuable.

Although, as it would turn out, from his perspective this was probably a poor decision.

TWENTY-SEVEN

'How does this look?'

It was the night of Linda's birthday party, the All Hallow's Eve's Eve Eve Eve shindig, with the possibility of a sleepover. Adam had forgotten that a costume was required until he received a text message from Aoife telling him that she was having difficulty finding the right wand. So, out of a sense of panic, he used scissors and an old greying bed sheet to create a makeshift costume at the last minute. After a few snips, a fake ghost stood in the mirror's reflection. I told him I was unimpressed and, to be honest, a little offended.

'How do you know what a ghost looks like? You can't see yourself in the mirror,' said Adam with an attitude that was not appreciated.

'I think you would have mentioned if I looked like a bedsheet.'

'That's very trusting of you,' he said with a smile that was sassier than I liked.

The thought that the thing I most resembled was vandalised linen concerned me, so I decided to take my mind off it and tease Adam by asking him if this special effect was from a particular movie.

'Oh, umm, one of the ones with a ghost? *A Christmas Carol*?'

'A what?'

'Oh, yeah, you wouldn't know what Christmas is.'

'Is it about not scary ghosts?'

'Fine,' he said, pulling the sheet off. 'It would be awkward anyway.'

I was a little pleased he took my considerations on board.

'Oh, I have an idea,' he said, running to his wardrobe and pulling out a Superman T-shirt, a shirt and a suit.

'You have a suit?'

'It was for my cousin Nicole's wedding,' he said, putting it on. He left the top couple of buttons of the shirt unbuttoned so you could see the T-shirt underneath.

'This kind of looks like Clark Kent mid-change into Superman, right?' said Adam. I had to admit, it was pretty clever.

'You need glasses,' I said.

He found some 3D glasses from the cinema in a drawer and cut out the lenses. Finally he combed his hair over for that clean-cut Superman look, then paused for a moment. His scar was on full display, for everyone to see.

'You know what, I've nothing to hide,' he said. 'MUM! I'M READY!'

'SURE, HONEY!' said his chauffeur, shouting from the living room downstairs. Adam's mother lived in a constant state of readiness when she was at home, in case her help was required in restoring her son back to the path of a normal life. This was handy for transportation purposes.

After some confusion over directions, we arrived at Linda's

house. It was a large place hidden behind trees. It looked nice, with an earnest decay I approved of. Linda opened the door, wearing her blonde hair in a long plait and a blue dress that trailed along the floor. She held a bag of ice cubes and handed one to Adam.

'Hello, Clark,' she said.

'Hello, Elsa.'

'Come in!' she sang.

Inside, the house was decorated with small lights on the walls and random lines of brightly coloured, reflective garlands sat on her parents' bookshelves, woven between novels and photos of her family: two parents and a sister and a brother I didn't know about. In the living room, which I presumed was the heart of the party since it contained the music and a silent black and white film playing as wallpaper, was the other guest who had arrived. It was Aoife, dressed in what I assumed was her school uniform (which looked surprisingly old-fashioned) and waving a stick.

'Hi, Clark,' said Aoife. 'Can I get a kiss from Superman?'

'Sure thing, ah …' said Adam, struggling to place her character, 'school goer?'

'School goer? I'll have you know I'm Hermione.'

Adam shrugged.

She shook her head with mock frustration and tapped Adam on the head with her stick. 'Oh, I read your new story. It was grim as usual.'

'Thank you, I think.'

Next Douglas arrived, his hair swept up into a voluminous quiff and wearing a T-shirt that informed the reader that meat was murder.

'I see the traitor is late. Not surprised; his timing was always off, just like his drumming.'

'Actually, I'm already here,' said Barry, who had customised his jumper into a Freddy Kruger costume, 'and I brought a friend.'

Douglas sniffed.

'I said it was okay,' said Linda, closing the door. 'This is … sorry, I've completely forgotten.'

'Andrew,' said Andrew, sticking his hand out to shake Douglas's hand.

'That's Adam. My name is of no purpose as I sincerely doubt I will speak to either you or Barry this evening,' Douglas harrumphed and walked past the two of them.

'Hi,' said Adam sheepishly.

'So go ahead to the TV room. I'll talk to Douglas. DOUG-LAS! YOU AREN'T RUINING MY PARTY.'

'I CAN RUIN AS I PLEASE!'

After Linda convinced Douglas to stop acting like such a prick, it was decided this would be a good time to start playing some party games. Linda was turning sixteen and she felt this was the perfect time to begin regressing to a more innocent time, so she brought out various old board games, although she did make the concession to her teenage years by introducing 'drinking cans' as an integral part of the rules.

I noticed a moment of slight panic in Adam's eyes when Douglas produced a white plastic bag filled with cans with Polish writing on them.

'Work away, gang,' said Douglas, 'I brought lots.'

Adam took the can given to him. He held it, testing its weight.

'You've never drunk one of these, have you?' I said.

'Shh!' he said to me and, with added resolve, pulled the tab on the top. Bubbles fizzled out and he sucked them up before they had a chance to dribble on the carpet. He gulped down the liquid with some surprise. Aoife saw this and laughed.

'Eh, this totally isn't the first time I've had alcohol,' he said with a slight smile.

'Oh dear,' she said, not believing him for a second, 'you've submitted to peer pressure.'

'Tsk tsk,' said Linda. 'In his defence, all the cool kids are doing it.'

'No doubt he will drop out of school now and join a motorcycle gang.'

'Truly I am a cautionary tale,' said Adam, who then took a big sip; too big, in fact, as he ended up coughing.

'Slow down, tiger,' said Douglas. 'No need to try and impress us.'

'Are your parents around?' Adam said.

'Nah, I'm having a family thing on my actual birthday on Tuesday. They went out for dinner and left my older brother in charge.'

'Oh, is he upstairs?'

'No, he went out, left me in charge.'

'Ah, it's a cool brother who believes in delegation.'

Music I recognised from a mobile phone ad began to play in the background and Linda jumped up on a chair.

'LADIES AND GENTLEMEN … and Douglas, this party has started! May the games begin!'

We started by playing a board game called Monopoly, which may be the dullest use of money possible. Aoife had a knack for it and soon was a clear captain of industry.

'I'm not playing this any more,' said Barry. 'I now hate capitalism.'

'Don't blame the market for your poor decisions in property investments,' said Aoife. 'Oh, Linda, I believe you owe me rent.'

'I'm with Barry. We need to seize the means of production and kick out ye corrupt landlords.'

'Excuse me, where's the bathroom?' said Andrew.

'Top of the stairs on the left,' said Linda.

'If I'm not back in ten minutes, I leave the waterworks to Barry.'

After Andrew got up and headed to the bathroom, Barry looked at us and raised his eyebrow. 'So what do you think of Andrew?'

'Tiresome,' said Douglas.

'He's very nice,' said Linda, ignoring this. 'Where did you find him?'

'The plank store?' said Douglas.

'I started talking to him online on Twitter. He could be it.'

'It?'

'You know, the second gay friend that the group has, so I can come out.'

'Um, I don't think he is too interested in being *our* friend,' said Aoife.

'What do you mean?'

This was true. Over the course of the game, Andrew had clearly been trying to ingratiate himself with the group, but was much more attentive to Barry than the others, following his every move. At one point, he didn't even collect rent when Barry landed on Mayfair.

'Barry, I think you may be on a date.'

Barry's eyes widened with fear and at the same time Douglas's lit up with delight. It was clear Barry was unprepared for this. Andrew returned from the bathroom and Douglas leapt up.

'Andrew, forgive me, I have been an outrageous cad. Please sit down. My name is Douglas.'

'Thank you,' said Andrew, perhaps hopeful the night was going his way.

'Everyone, I am going to the fridge. People need any top-ups? I think there are only four cans left but Barry and Andrew can share, right?'

Andrew nodded as Barry flushed with embarrassment.

'How about a different game?' said Aoife, trying to change the subject.

'How about Twister? I bet you're flexible, Andrew.'

'Eh, um, how about … Game of Life?' said Barry.

'It's a spooky night. How about Bloody Mary?' said Andrew. 'See what ghosts are in the house?'

There was a sharp intake of breath from everyone but Adam and Linda. Andrew, suddenly sensing an invisible line had been crossed, began to retreat. 'Actually, it's not that spooky a night. I made a mistake. I think …'

Linda exhaled through her nose. I was not clear about what was going on and I don't think Adam was either.

'No, no. I want to play it. We should play it. What are the rules?'

'Linda, we don't have to,' said Aoife.

'No, I want to. This is what normal teenagers do at parties. I want to play it.'

Andrew coughed, the unwelcome centre of attention. 'Ah, basically you stand in front of the bathroom mirror repeating the phrase Bloody Mary in the bathroom mirror. Apparently if you say it four times in a mirror, some dead girl shows up to bother you.'

'We can all fit in the upstairs bathroom,' said Linda.

As it turns out, you could comfortably fit about twenty people in there. Linda obviously came from a well-off family. We all stared at the mirror. Everyone stood there waiting for the cue. Linda began and everyone followed.

'Bloody Mary,' said the uncertain chorus.

'Bloody Mary.'

'Bloody … Mary.'

'Bloo …'

Linda broke down, tears pouring down her face. I'm not sure if she said anything or was simply making inarticulate sobs of no particular words.

'It's okay,' said Aoife, 'you don't have to prove anything. We're here.'

'It's not fair,' she sobbed, I think.

Adam placed a comforting hand on her shoulder but he didn't know its purpose. Poor Andrew stood in the corner, terrified about what a bad turn his night had taken.

'Sorry, can I have a second?' Linda said and everyone filed out and moved back downstairs. On the way down, Adam noticed more photographs of the sister Linda had never mentioned and who hadn't attended the party. I can guess what her name was.

A few minutes later, Linda came back downstairs with puffy red eyes. 'So, what do people want to do now?'

Adam stood up. 'I would like to suggest that we drink more cans and watch movies.'

'I knew I was friends with you for a reason.'

So the remainder of the night was spent watching horror movies, *The Sixth Sense*, *The Conjuring* and *Gremlins* in the TV room. Adam was sipping on his second can of beer and he was not proving to be a natural drinker. I wondered if he feared its dark powers, which we learned about in school and on TV. Either that or he just didn't like the taste. I think it was something of a relief when Linda's parents texted that they were coming home and there was a scramble to dispose of the evidence of underage boozing, before resuming horror watching.

By the time the last film in the marathon, *IT*, had ended, everyone had cocooned themselves into sleeping bags on the TV room floor and snores were emanating from everyone except Aoife. She was wide awake and appeared to be thinking intensely about something. I wondered what she was thinking. I could easily tell what Adam had on his mind, but I spend ninety-nine per cent of my existence with him. I don't know anything much about other people.

Suddenly she gave a decisive nod. With her sleeping bag zipped up to her neck, she sat up and fell gently on her front. She scrunched forward like a caterpillar until she reached Adam. They had been on separate sides of the room, due to a strict 'No Hanky Panky' rule from Linda.

'Adam?' she whispered. When he didn't respond with more than a faint snore, she pulled her arm out of the bag and poked him in the cheek.

'Mmmm?' he mmmmed.

'Are you awake?' she whispered.

'Yes?'

She smiled nervously. 'Sorry to wake you. Did you know about Linda's sister?'

'No. No one told me.'

'Yeah, it was a car accident, about four years ago.'

'I'm really glad I didn't dress as a ghost now.'

'It's okay. It's not a secret or anything, but she doesn't like to talk about it.'

'Did you wake me to talk to me about people not talking?'

'Oh, yeah, no. I was thinking since you told me everything about your problems …'

He nodded. This wasn't quite true as he sure as shit hadn't mentioned me. Aoife swallowed. 'Adam, I want to talk to you about my mum soon.'

'Your mum? Eh, sure.'

'Great!'

Aoife kissed him and then lay down, her sleeping bag next to his. Then they proceeded to fall asleep, the two of them snug as bugs.

III

AIN'T NO CURE FOR LOVE

TWENTY-EIGHT

The morning ritual of pulling books from lockers perplexed me a little. Not how people do it (I do understand how lockers work), but the amount of time people spend doing it. Really at most it should take you two minutes to locate your geography book. But instead, they take ages to find one thing.

Adam was retrieving his business studies book slowly as two classmates talked next to him.

'I dunno,' said the one called Rickie.

'I'm telling you, baiy, you wanna get that under control,' said Kieran, the other one. 'I've the one and I'm happy. You don't want the two lays wrecking your head. What do you think?'

It took Adam a couple of seconds to register that they were talking to him, including him.

'Rickie here is seeing two old dolls and can't decide which one to choose.'

'Eh, whichever one you like the most?' Adam said.

'Easy for you to say, your one is a ride,' said Rickie. 'Balls, that's the bell. Later.'

'Later.'

'Later?' said Adam.

I had noticed that since the appearance of Aoife at the school gates, Adam's fellow students were a bit less distant. They weren't coming over to the house with flowers or anything, but his cachet had certainly risen among the ranks. I would suggest that this was very shallow of them, that his popularity depended on his ability to have an attractive girlfriend, but I guess they didn't know him. If he had a girl, this was something that they could relate to, rather than thinking of him as the 'attempt to kill self with hammer' boy.

***

At lunchtime, Adam was told to go to the principal's office. He hadn't done anything wrong as far as he was aware, but still worried about it as we walked down the corridor to the office. On the way I admired the Christmas decorations that were littering the wall. I had only just learned about Christmas and it sounded bizarre. Trees indoors, plants to kiss under, songs about kings and gentlemen and being cold outside.

Adam knocked on the door.

'Come in,' called Mr O'Neill.

'You wanted to see me?'

Despite being quite thin, the principal projected a width that made him fearsome. 'Please sit,' he said. 'Adam, as we are approaching the Christmas holidays I wanted to have a little chat.'

'Okay.'

'Really, I just wanted to congratulate you on the great strides you are making. I've noticed your grades have improved and your teachers tell me you are being more responsive and getting on with classmates much better.'

'Thank you?'

This was true. Adam now had all the things that happy, successful people have. He had a hobby, he had a circle of friends, a girlfriend even, someone to talk to about his troubles. (In one of the writing group evenings, I can't remember which one as they all blended into one, *Niamh* said that the key to drama is conflict. No one wants a story about people having a grand old time, since it's boring. And she's right. Let's just say the weeks between Halloween and December were full of uneventful bliss.)

'You should be very proud. I appreciate how tough it is to keep things on an even keel.'

'What's an even keel?' I asked.

'Especially with all the messy business with Chris.'

The principal put out his hand to shake. Adam, a little confused, put his out to join it.

'Oh, and I have some good news!' Mr O'Neill continued.

'Mmm?'

'We've set a date for the mental health seminar. We've arranged a whole day of talks and events for the students to really get to grips with the difficult issues of mental health. We even have a musician coming in.'

He mentioned a name, but I had no idea who he was referring to.

'Uh, very good, sir. When is it?'

'January. You know, new year, new start. We are going to film it, put it on the Internet, really reach people, maybe even make the school go "viral",' he said, using his fingers as quotation marks.

'Very exciting.'

'If it goes right, we'll make some major steps to avoiding more … incidents,' he said, carefully choosing the word so as not to offend Adam.

'Sounds good,' said Adam, letting his principal off.

'Yes it does.' As he stood, the bell rang. 'Ah, it's time for you to return to class. Oh, I think I see Philip waiting. He's my next appointment. He has taken his brother's death very hard, you know. Can't imagine … anyway … Hello, Philip, I was just telling Adam here about our mental health event.'

Philip clearly didn't think that this was good news, but he said nothing and merely nodded. As he stared at Adam, his face turned an odd shade of red, as if someone was slowly pouring a carton of cranberry juice into a human-head-shaped jug. Adam smiled nervously.

'At any rate, come in, Philip. Adam, I'll talk to you anon.'

As he walked past, Philip bumped him in the shoulder, unbalancing Adam a little.

'Sorry,' said Philip, insincerely.

Mr O'Neill shut his door behind them and Adam wandered down the corridor. 'Wait, which class is next?'

I informed him I wasn't his timetable, so he pulled out his journal and checked. Geography.

'Balls, I left the book in my locker.'

Adam ran to the hall where the lockers lived. On the way

he ran into a classmate dossing off a class, who nodded at him. How curious that Adam was now worthy of notice. Moving on, Adam found and opened his locker. As he pulled out his book, a piece of paper fluttered out of the locker and fell softly to the floor. Adam picked it up and opened it.

'What do you and a nail have in common? You usually need a couple of swings of the hammer to do the job. Shame.'

That joke was terrible – whoever wrote it needed to work on his punchline. Adam also didn't laugh. In fact he didn't say anything. He just stared at it.

'Adam, shouldn't you be in class?' said a passing teacher.

'Oh, yes, sir. I forgot my book.'

He crumpled up the piece of paper and threw it back into his locker.

TWENTY-NINE

Ding.

After six stops, the bus slowed to a halt and Adam and Aoife got off. Ballincollig was an unfamiliar place to Adam. In fact, as near as I could tell, being on a bus was an unfamiliar experience for Adam. Such was the existence of the city boy apparently. Everyone came to you, rather than you going to them. It cost nearly €4 one way to get to this stop, but he didn't know if that was standard or not. He still complained about it.

'So this is your street?'

Adam was nervous about ever meeting her mother, and doubly so since Aoife had told him about her problems. However, he didn't say this, and when she suggested he come to her place after the writing group one evening, he felt it would be unboyfriendlike to refuse.

'It's a nice area. Lots of trees.'

'It's pretty boring. We do have many, many supermarkets, though.'

They walked along and, every step they got closer, it was clear that Aoife was becoming more and more unsettled. Eventually they got to her house, an unremarkable two-storey building with an overgrown lawn.

'You ready?' said Aoife.

'Ready teddy!' said Adam. He was attempting to lighten the mood, but he was as nervous as Aoife.

'Oh, I forgot my keys!' Aoife looked around and picked up a pot next to the door, revealing a house key. She gave Adam a conspiratorial look. 'Tell no one.'

Aoife opened the door to her house and called, 'Mum?'

'Yes?'

'Dad home?'

'No. Your father is still at work. A meeting with a client overran apparently.'

Aoife's mum appeared. She was a little shorter than her daughter, so she had to tilt her head up to speak to her.

'Hello, Mrs Callaghan,' said Adam.

'Oh, you must be the young man that Aoife is always talking about,' she said.

'Mum!'

'Well, her father is not home yet so I will go get some milk,' she said, leaving the room. I wondered if milk and her father not being home were somehow connected? She walked with an uncertain step, as if a nervousness was built in.

'I don't talk about you that much,' said Aoife. 'She is confusing you with a different Adam I talk way more about.'

'I'm sure,' said Adam, grinning.

Mrs Callaghan returned holding a jug of milk and three glasses. She poured it out for the three of them and sat. Adam drank a sip of the milk and waited for the conversation to start.

'So, how was your day, Mum?'

'I went to town.'

'Oh, we were just in town.'

'Yes, we were, Mrs Callaghan. We were just at our writing thing. Aoife had written an amazing poem about a zombie who had fallen in love with an mannequin. Everyone thought it was funny, even that girl with the weird laugh whose name I can never remember but sounds like–'

Aoife grabbed his hand and squeezed it hard, indicating that he was perhaps going a bit far.

'That's nice,' said her mother, with a little, uncomfortable smile. The next thing she said was a question in her own language. Aoife responded in the same language, of which Adam and I understood nothing, but I sensed it held disapproval of suddenly switching language in the company of guests. Suddenly Aoife said Adam's name and they both looked back at him.

'Oh, ah, would it be okay if I used the bathroom?'

It would be a relief to get out of the room. Mrs Callaghan said, 'It's at the top of the staircase on the left when you go past the books.'

He finished his business and washed his hands. I noticed the cabinet above the sink was open a crack.

'Go on. Have a look. Let's find out what secrets lurk in the House of Tuffour-Callaghan.'

He rolled his eyes but still he opened the cabinet. Gels, ointments, spare toothbrushes and loads of boxes of pills. It was like a pharmacy in there. (We looked the names up later. They were pretty powerful anti-anxiety medicines.)

On leaving the bathroom, Adam noticed a half-open door across the hall. He peered in and could see it was Aoife's room. It was oddly thrilling, sneaking around in someone else's house. The room was an astounding mess. The floor was covered with loose sheets of paper, clothes and books. She had posters up of bands I didn't recognise but I assumed from the gory depictions of some hell that they weren't country music.

'You need more skulls in your room,' I said to Adam.

'I'm all right, thanks.'

'Aren't you going to head in?'

He shook his head.

Lame, I thought.

Adam walked back downstairs and there was a beep from his phone. It was a text message from his dad asking if he would be home for dinner, but no rush.

'Do you need to go?' said Aoife.

'Ah … no.'

'Good, he can stay for dinner,' said Aoife's mother.

He texted back, 'At Aoife's. Will be fed here.'

A text pinged back immediately. 'OK, enjoy meeting the in-laws.'

That was it. We were stuck there for the evening.

There was the sound of keys rattling and a door opening in the hall.

'Is that your father? He told me he was stuck in a meeting and would be late.'

'No, it's your most handsome son,' responded a voice, the owner of which stepped into the living room.

'Josh!' said Aoife.

'Joshua!' said her mother. 'You're supposed to be in Galway.'

'I thought I'd pay a visit to my dear old family for the weekend. Hello mother, hey sis and … new friend.'

'Hi,' Adam said.

'Oh, yes, Adam, this is my brother Josh. Josh, this is Adam, my friend, boy, boyfriend.'

'Ah, got another one caught in your web, eh, Afs?'

'He's joking. I don't have a web. I don't date that many–'

'It's cool. I'm not judging. One, uh, should have many, eh … amours.'

Joshua started to laugh. 'This one is funny! What's for dinner?'

'Oh, I'm not sure.'

'I'll start it, give you a break for once Afs. How does Thai sound?'

'I'm not sure if we have the ingredients.'

'Worry not,' he said, opening his bag and pouring out an impressive collection of ingredients. 'There was a flood in the local speciality shop and a box floated by our house. We have a year's worth of glass noodles.'

He dashed into the kitchen, grabbed a wok and got started.

Dinner passed smoothly enough and it was agreed that Joshua made a delicious meal. Aoife and Joshua could talk forever, and at length they caught the table up with the minutiae of their lives. All in all, it was a fairly pleasant experience. Aoife's mother seemed a touch eccentric, but nothing too shocking.

'So how do you two know each other?' Josh asked, setting his fork down on an empty plate.

'Oh, we're in the same writing group.'

'You're a writer too? What's your bag? Funny stuff, sci-fi?'

'Oh, he writes–'

'Afs, I'm sure he can answer for himself.'

'Ah, I guess drama. Some is a little horror-y.'

'That's cool, although, man, I can't read any of that stuff. Gives me the creeps if there is a zombie or even a spider.'

'I never understand why Aoife writes so much about ghosts and ghouls,' said Mrs Callaghan. 'Life is frightening enough without adding to it. I read one the other day that was about a man stabbed in a basement.'

'Mum! I didn't show you that one!'

'You left it on the table.'

'Yeah, in a notebook marked "DON'T READ, MUM!"'

'It's not good to be reading stories like that, or writing them.'

'I can write what I like!'

In response, Mrs Callaghan didn't say anything, but instead starting breathing in and out very quickly.

'MUM!' said Aoife. 'Please don't do this.'

Her mother clutched her chest and began to tremble. 'My own daughter. She shouts at me. She doesn't love me.'

'Mum, you know I love you. I …'

Mrs Callaghan was now moaning and rocking in her chair.

'Should I call someone?' Adam said, getting up.

'No, it's okay. I'll talk her down,' said Josh. 'Aoife, why don't you walk Adam to the bus stop.'

'Thank you for the dinner, Josh.'

Her brother gave him a thumbs up. 'It's all right. Next time, you'll have to tell me the story behind your gnarly scar.'

They walked out the door and there was an unusual silence between them, and not a comfortable one either. Adam wanted to ask something, but he did not know the best route, and Aoife looked like she wanted to answer it but found an invisible roadblock stopping her.

Eventually, 'Will your mother be okay?'

'Yeah, she'll be fine. If she finds things stressful, she has panic attacks. It's my fault. I shouldn't have snapped at her about the stories–'

'No, no, I shouldn't have stayed for dinner, you did warn me a bit and–'

'You're too sweet. And besides, she asked you to stay. She seemed okay. I think having everyone there was just too much.'

'Oh,' Adam said.

'I … I shouldn't have brought you here,' said Aoife.

'No, it's okay. Are you all right?' Adam said.

'Oh, it will be fine. Josh is here,' said Aoife.

'Sure? Shit, that's my bus.'

'We'll talk about it later!' said Aoife, kissing Adam on the cheek. Adam stuck out his hand to flag down the bus and then almost flew through the door in his eagerness to get away.

As the bus headed back into the city, he sat in an empty back seat and stared out the window, watching the passing trees turn into the bright windows of the city centre.

***

Later that evening Adam received an email from Aoife and it was pretty long. Writers don't half go on. I would suggest if you have a burning desire to date a writer type, go for a poet. Poems tend to be shorter and it's easier to pretend that they are any good.

Hi Adam!

Sorry about earlier. I find these kinds of things difficult to talk about so I have cut and pasted a story I wrote a long time ago. I don't know if it's very good and it's definitely not as fun as the usual (so your kind of tale!) but it's heavily based on the truth:

One Monday morning, Amy decided going to school was not something she wanted to do. However she had a cunning plan: if she hid underneath her blanket and avoided detection, if she stayed in bed and no one noticed, she wouldn't have to go. She grabbed her light-up Pokémon clock and covered herself with her duvet.

8.32. 8.33. 8.34.

She was getting away with it, she realised, she had outfoxed her mother! It didn't matter that she had attempted this on at least a dozen different occasions and each time had failed miserably. Finally it was going to work.

8.45. 8.46. 8.47. This was usually the time her mother had her in the car on the way.

She had done it! But rather than be cocky, she stayed in bed, reading Skulduggery Pleasant. *She read until she noticed that it was 10.12. It was odd that she had heard no sign of Mum. She didn't want to go to school but she wanted to know where Mum was, so a stealth mission was required. She got out of bed and snuck around. No Mum in the kitchen, no Mum in the TV room, no Mum in the bathroom.*

She tiptoed to her parents' bedroom and slowly pushed open the door and peered in.

Her mum was hiding under her blanket too.

Her mum was a strange woman, but Amy didn't know why until that day. Before then, Amy knew she was not like the other mothers in the school yard, but she assumed it was because she didn't come from here. Perhaps there was a town of women like her somewhere else. Quirky ladies that felt things more strongly than here.

She looked so sad underneath the blanket but Amy wasn't sure what to do, so she went to the kitchen to make her favourite meal, but she didn't know what that was, since she rarely ate dinner at the same time as Mum and Dad. So she made Corn Flakes instead.

Amy brought it up to her Mum and gave it to her, but she didn't respond. She just stared at Amy and looked sad. When Dad came home from work some hours later, he saw that Amy was still in her pyjamas.

'Where's your mother?' he said.

'In bed.'

He nodded and disappeared to their room. When he returned an hour later, he made Amy dinner, something he never did.

'Amy, I'm afraid your mother is very sad.'

And that's how I learned that my mother got sad.

Sorry, I don't have a better ending.

A xxx

P.S. *Spiderman* during the week?

THIRTY

The problem with being a ghost – actually there are many problems: being a ghost is pretty crap – but probably the main one is that there are not many activities you can partake in. Football, knitting and dressage are all completely out of the question for the physically non-present. However, there is one thing I can enjoy without the aid of a body: books.

It began when we started writing. It seemed important to read more to improve our writing. And, man, I fell for it. Movies were okay, but I spend the majority of my day watching people. With books, I could see inside people instead.

I loved nothing more than reading, which was a problem, as it was a love I had no control over. I was completely at the mercy of Adam's reading habits. Since I could not turn pages or lift books or anything, I had to stand behind Adam as he read. This was initially fine. Adam and I read at the same pace and had similar tastes in stories.

Unfortunately, when he became 'Adam & Aoife' they began swapping books, and she had terrible taste in books – nothing but nonsensical fantasy; novels which all seemed to have the same plot about castles and magic, chosen boys and their quest to be as amazing as everyone says they are. On the way boy meets girl, who is good with a bow and arrow and protecting her family from the evil Celtic-sounding-named one, and who realises this young man's potential and bleurgh.

One day, I requested we read something else and Adam nodded. He held up the next book and considered it. 'It's supposed to be good.'

'We've read about nothing but bloody wizards for the last month. Can we read something with real people in it?'

'I don't have any of those at the moment.'

I think he sensed my annoyance.

'Shall we write something instead?

'Are you going to continue ignoring my suggestions?'

'What do you mean?'

We had started writing a story a few days earlier and he had resisted my points and ideas for no reason. This wouldn't bother me except that they were plainly more interesting than the sentimental, gooey rubbish that he was presently writing. Awful muck, but he persisted in writing it! It was offensive to read and I know he was only writing it because he thought it was something he should be writing, since he was in a relationship. As I was in a bad mood, I decided to bring this to his attention.

'Sentimental?'

'Yeah, it's all about the main character fancying a girl. It's lame.'

'The stories can't be depressing all the time.'

'They should be if the alternative is as bad as this.'

Adam went red at this remark. 'Well go write your own story so! Oh yeah, that's right, you can't!'

'You don't want to get on the wrong side of me, ADAM.'

'Or what? Are you going to float ominously at me until I die? I'm trembling.'

'We'll see if your girlfriend will still want you after she reads your terrible story.'

'PISS OFF! WHY ARE YOU STILL HERE?'

My imaginary heart burned with a real pain, a righteous anger. He despised me. I had helped him move on, forced him out of this horrible room, and now he was leaving me for his new life of friends and sun and books about warlocks throwing clouds at each other.

I saw his face. He regretted making that wounding comment.

'I'm sorry about that.'

'It's okay.'

It wasn't.

'Do you want to look at the story again?'

'Sure.'

We worked on the story for the next hour and Adam went to bed satisfied with it. It was less terrible, it's true.

When he fell asleep, I went to town, but I felt too stricken to enjoy it. I couldn't hear the buzz of the lamps or the revelry of the night owls.

Stupid Adam.

THIRTY-ONE

In school, during sex education, Adam was told of the importance of protection. (The official line was that the best protection was abstinence, but the SPHE teacher giving the talk had long abandoned any illusions that a herd of teenage boys had any self control, so he thought they should at least wear a condom.) Adam, having not been in a relationship of any length to my knowledge, decided it was prudent to have a condom on his person in case the situation suddenly called for one (I thought he was being wildly optimistic). He even bought a new wallet since his old one didn't have a secret sleeve to hide it in, and so his one stolen condom hid in this pocket until one evening in December.

One Saturday evening he left the house, shouting goodbye to his parents, but instead of going towards the city he slipped around the house to his back yard. A moment later he snuck past the end of the house and walked quickly towards a green area with a little enclave of trees. Sitting in the centre was a fully erect tent. Aoife popped her head out.

'It's me,' she said.

'Hello, I'm excited to be here at "the cinema".'

'Oh, there's a strong alibi. How did you explain the sleeping bags?' she said pointing at the two underneath his arm, as he pushed his way into the tent.

'I hid them in the shed last week.'

'How cunning.'

They kissed.

Aoife moved back, which made a clinking noise.

'What's that noise?'

She pulled out a bottle of red wine, a corkscrew and two glasses. 'My parents have a large collection they never touch. I don't think they'll miss it.'

'Handy, we have none in my house.'

'Not big drinkers?'

Since the incident, Adam's parents had made sure that there wasn't a drop of alcohol in the house, in case it would someday be used to facilitate a second attempt – the literature described it as 'a known depressant'.

'Yeah. But don't worry, I did not come empty-handed,' he said patting his bag. (Spoiler: it held some cheese and two packets of salt and vinegar Taytos.)

And so they prepared. Two sleeping bags were zipped together to form one mega sleeping bag and they arranged Christmas lights inside the tent.

'Why the lights?' said Adam.

'When I go camping, I want to look up and see the stars. Except you can't see them in the city, so these will have to do,' said Aoife. He kissed her on the cheek and complimented her cleverness. The way to the woman's heart must be through the brain as this was met with a kiss on the lips, mouths open.

Adam pulled back and then took the cheese out of his bag. He had gone for a variety. Block of cheddar, EasiSingles and some Cheesestrings. He offered them on a plate.

'Cheese and wine, this is what grown-ups do,' said Aoife, peeling off a layer of Cheesestring with her front teeth.

'Yes, I'm sure they do it in tents in the woods too,' said Adam, laughing nervously. He felt he was on the cusp of a seminal moment and didn't know whether he needed to chase it or wait for it, or maybe even run away.

'If they don't, they should.'

They kissed again. This time it went on longer, with hands travelling underneath several layers of clothing. (Erotic atmosphere or not, it was still December in Ireland.) When they stopped again, Aoife opened the wine, a 2014 Chilean red, and poured it unevenly between the two glasses. They raised their glasses and clinked them. Adam laughed at nothing, took a sip and nearly gagged.

'You, sir, are not the wine connoisseur you made yourself out to be.'

'I am afraid that I have deceived you, my dear.'

'I could never love a man who does not love wine. For that man has no soul.'

Aoife took a gulp and also did not seem keen. At least, I could assume so, as a little bit came back out, pouring down the side of her lips.

'Good year?'

'Quiet, you.'

They both took another sip.

'The taste is better when you get used to it.'

'Have you had wine before?'

Adam scratched his neck and decided to not lie. 'No. This is my first time. You?'

Aoife put down her glass. 'Only once. Oh, I have my iPod. Should I put on something romantic?' she asked with a raised eyebrow.

'You have something romantic on it?'

Aoife scrolled through her list. 'Define "romantic".'

Adam stole a kiss on her cheek, and she retaliated with her mouth and things escalated. She dropped her iPod. Adam spilled his wine, spoiling his T-shirt. (He would later throw it out to avoid detection.) Aoife's solution to this was to remove the T-shirt and, so that he didn't feel embarrassed, she removed hers as well.

'Hey, do you want to?' said Aoife.

'Sure, why not,' he said nervously.

'Do you have a thingy?'

'I thought it was pretty obvious. Oh wait, you mean …'

Adam crawled back to his jacket and pulled out his wallet. At last! He found the secret sleeve that held the thingy – the square of silver foil.

'A gentleman is always prepared!'

He tried tearing the foil, but the sweat on his fingers meant that his fingers slipped with each attempt. Eventually he decided to tear it open with his teeth – perhaps he hoped the effect would be that of a wild, insatiable animal, ready to ravish its prey. Aoife laughed instead.

He pulled the clear plastic thingy from within and then looked at it. With horror, he realised that he didn't know how to use it.

'Is there a particular side you have to use?'

Aoife looked at it. 'I don't think it matters, unless it's one of those fancy ones.'

Adam froze, probably recalling deciding between 'Double Strength' and 'Ribbed for Her Pleasure' from his parents' drawer. He'd decided on Double Strength, since safety comes first and he didn't really want to think about the other one. (He didn't appreciate my remark that his parents had a well stocked and varied selection.)

'Do you have data?' said Adam. 'I'll google it.'

'My mother watches my Internet history like a hawk. There is no way you're looking it up on my phone.'

'Well then, mmm, chancing it is probably not a good idea …'

'It's not.'

'Sorry about this. I should have read the instructions.'

'It's okay. We could just do other stuff; other stuff is fun.'

I'm going to stop describing now as I don't know the logistics and, to be honest, I stopped watching. After they were finished, they lay there in their combined sleeping bag, their faces illuminated by their rows of mock stars.

'Other stuff is fun.'

'Told ya,' said Aoife.

In the distance, there was a difficult to identify noise, maybe a scream, maybe a car. Adam jerked up and looked towards it.

'Banshee!' said Aoife.

'A what?'

'A banshee? Surely you know what a banshee is?'

Adam coughed. 'Is it a fox?'

Aoife laughed and began to explain what it was. Back in the time of fairies and mermen and little green men jealously guarding their gold, the oldest families of Ireland had a ghost that was passed down from generation to generation. This ghost was always a female and it either looked like a beautiful dainty thing or a wizened old hag and it never spoke. It only screamed.

'What did it sound like?'

'Well, according to one book, one Frenchman copied it down on paper when he heard it in Argentina, visiting his friend. You can play it on the violin!'

'Why does it appear?'

'The banshee only appears for one reason. It's there to tell you that a relative is going to die.'

'Like a warning?'

'No, a certainty,' Aoife said gravely, before she broke into a smile. Adam didn't smile though.

'Aoife, do you believe in the supernatural?'

'Like banshees?'

'No, I mean, like ghosts.'

She thought about this for a moment.

'I don't know. Sometimes,' she said thoughtfully. 'I think there are many things we don't understand and because we don't, we pretend they don't exist. People prefer it.'

They were silent for a moment. I saw his arm crush her belly gently.

'What about you?' she said.

'What about me?'

'Do you believe in ghosts?'

Adam's eyes groped in the darkness, looking for me but I don't think he found me. He didn't answer her question and, instead, kissed her again.

I wandered away. I could see that he didn't miss me, didn't need me. I didn't know what to do so I went somewhere else, somewhere familiar. It wasn't until later that I realised I had walked away while he was awake.

*****

Philip didn't sleep in his own room. In secret, he slept in his brother's room, which remained the same as it was when Chris officially checked out.

Chris had been the kind of guy who would be polite about everything. If something seemingly inconsequential bothered him, he wouldn't bother other people with it. In retrospect that was the problem. But Chris made it seem so effortless. He wore his charisma like a shield, deflecting all the world's troubles. Perhaps, Philip thought, it was the same shield that trapped everything in. Maybe he was trying to understand someone he apparently did not know at all.

I don't remember going to his house. I wasn't thinking and found myself standing outside and saw that a light was on. There were no Christmas decorations, the only house in its row with no tree in the window. I passed through the kitchen, where his parents were eating take-out, and went upstairs to Chris's old room, where once again I found Philip. This wasn't the first time I had been here.

He was sitting on the bed, holding his brother's old school blazer. Carefully he examined every pocket and fold in it. He held it up to the lamplight. It was lightly worn in places, but was well kept. Philip looked at it for a few moments and then, in a moment of violence, stood up and attempted to rip it apart. Starting at the collar, he pulled and pulled. It made a minor rip, and with the slight tearing noise, his strength appeared to vanish and he dropped it. He began to cry, the kind of full-on tears that only happen when you know that no one is watching. He kicked the blazer away and lay down on the bed.

I drifted back outside. Night had begun to lose its allure. What once was exciting and vibrant had become tired and rundown. It was the same streets, the same people, the same rot. I didn't understand these people. I lived outside their lives, their hopes, theirs dreams. They have such big emotions. Anger, fear, love.

No one loved me. I hoped Adam would, but he didn't. He tolerated me, at best. He loved Aoife, or at least was in the beginnings of such a state. Now I knew what it looked like, I could see that I didn't have that.

People make a mistake about love. They think it's a gift, something that enters your life to lighten the load. It's not, though. It's a sense of obligation that ties two people together. This isn't a gift. It's an anchor and if you aren't big enough, anchors can make you sink.

I returned to the tent and waited outside. They were being cute and listening to songs from her iPod, made worse by the tinny sound of their speakers. Their silhouettes made curious shapes. All shifting shadows, like some multi-limbed beast from some hell dimension.

A rumble in the air signalled the arrival of rain. It fell and they laughed like idiots as it bashed against their flimsy tent. They were happy.

I missed the old days, when it was just me and Adam. It wasn't, like, amazing, but at least I had someone I could talk to, someone to feel connected to, and we were getting on pretty well for a while. It's not fair that other people could take that away from me.

It was at this moment I decided that things had to go back to the way they used to be. That meant Aoife and his other friends had to go.

THIRTY-TWO

Of course, as a non-physical being, my options for separating Adam and his friends were limited. The problem with cunning plans of destruction is that they require a cunning plan of destruction, of which I had none. I thought it over for a few days. That he didn't ask why I was so quiet, or appear to notice my lack of engagement, further convinced me that my decision was the right one. We were never going to be pals with them around.

My first cunning plan was pretty simple. I would position myself at the top of the stairs, hiding behind the banister, and the moment he stepped on the rickety top step, I would shout 'Boo!' If I did it loud enough, he would be frightened, miss his footing and fall down the steps and break his leg at the bottom. This way he would be stuck in the hospital again with me. It was even possible that if we were in there long enough Aoife and his friends would forget about him all together.

In practice, however, that did not happen. One morning I made a most horrifying howl, but instead of a terrified tumble, he barely grunted and continued down to the kitchen.

'Blaa!'

I pulled a face while he made a sandwich in the hope that he would accidentally cut his hand in half instead of the bread. He just looked at me and shook his head. (This was an optimistic plan anyway since his mother had hidden any cutlery sharper than a banana as a precaution.)

It was clear pretty quickly that this plan to injure him wasn't going to work.

'Adam, are you going to town?' called his mother from upstairs.

'Sure.'

She pounded down the stairs and handed him a list from the fridge door. 'Could you pick these up?'

'This is, uh, a comprehensive list.'

Adam grabbed a bag for life and strolled out the door. 'You're in a weird mood, Casper,' he said as I attempted to scare him onto the road into oncoming traffic. I can't say I liked this new nickname, but at least he was noticing me.

'You know, being a ghost I'm supposed to scare things,' I said, but his attention had already turned to his phone. From a seat outside the café by Barrack Street (how many cafés are there in this town?) Linda waved him down.

'Hey, dreamer!' she said, covertly rolling a rollie in her lap. That could be the answer! Maybe Aoife didn't like smokers? Granted I never saw her disapprove of Linda's smoking but I'm sure it can't be pleasant to kiss a mouth reeking of ash and nicotine.

'You should get into smoking,' I said.

'What? No. My family has a weakness in the lungs.'

I sighed. For a kid who once rammed a blunt tool into the front of his brain, he was surprisingly health conscious.

Giving up, I watched him sit down and listened to them talk about getting a gift for Aoife for Christmas.

'You should give her a pair of smelly socks,' I suggested, 'or half a worm.' He pointedly ignored these suggestions.

'Cannibal Corpse is playing in Dublin in January,' said Linda.

'Oh, I could get tickets and we could take the bus up.'

'That sounds lovely! That is top boyfriending, sir.'

After this riveting conversation and a trip to the shop, we headed home again. Up in his room I stared out the window and plotted. I was so distracted by my plotting that I didn't notice for several minutes that he was writing something without me. A story! Without me! I told him I was appalled and sickened.

'It's not a story. Remember, Dr Moore said it might be helpful to start writing a journal on my feelings. I was going to ask you but asking the voice in your head for writing advice didn't seem a great start for a mental health diary.'

Even though I was insulted by this continuing insinuation that I was not real, I read over his shoulder. It was actually pretty good, but I wouldn't give him the satisfaction of telling him so. I missed the days when he was depressed, when I was literally the only person he said anything to. With any luck, I thought, he would get glum again, and I was going to do my best to help get him there.

THIRTY-THREE

Even as a ghost, it took ages to get out to Ballincollig. Also I couldn't quite remember the way, so I had to go into town and follow the bus route. On the way I could see Christmas was in full bloom. Lights and trees littered the streets, and crowds ambled around stalls selling small decorations, fast food and roasted chestnuts. There was a large wheel on the street, giving lovers an opportunity to see the whole city centre at once at an intoxicating height.

I was worried that I would be too late and everyone would be gone to bed, but fortunately the light was on. Aoife was sitting at the desk in her room, writing and listening to music on her headphones.

I'm not being a creep: I was there to uncover any skeletons in her closet. (There weren't any: just long jackets and black skirts.) The problem with Adam was he could only see her good points, but of course no one is perfect. So I selflessly decided to investigate, in order to reveal her most hideous character flaws.

I was hoping for something scandalous like another boyfriend or a secret arsenal of weapons but there was nothing very promising in her room. It was still a mess, the floor carpeted with pages that had notes and stories scribbled on them, and her clothes hanging randomly over furniture throughout.

I looked over her shoulder to see what she was writing. On the top it said 'MY AMAZING UNTITLED NOVEL'. The notes described a heroine who can't get into a posh wizard school. She is very frustrated, as the boy she fancies can, but later she uncovers the school's dastardly plan to turn their students into an evil army who will take over the magic world. The page was littered with doodles of school crests and wands. In a corner I could see a scribbled likeness of Adam in a wizard cloak with a demon following him and herself fighting it off. Had she figured it out?

'AOIFE, ARE YOU ASLEEP YET?' her mother shouted from downstairs.

'YES!'

'THAT DOESN'T MAKE SENSE!'

'I KNOW. WHY ARE YOU ASKING?'

'JUST TO TELL YOU YOU SHOULD BE ASLEEP. YOU HAVE SCHOOL TOMORROW.'

'I KNOW.'

'YOU SHOULD GO TO SLEEP.'

'NIGHT, MUM!'

'GOOD NIGHT!'

Aoife returned to her notes, shaking her head, and continued to write. Looking at her pages of writings, I was struck by how clear and legible her handwriting was in comparison to the chaos she surrounded herself with.

'AOIFE!'

'YES?'

'SORRY, I FORGOT WHAT I WAS GOING TO SAY.'

'NIGHT, MUM!'

'AOIFE! I JUST REMEMBERED. YOU HAVE TO BE ASLEEP BECAUSE YOUR UNCLE AND COUSIN ARE ARRIVING TOMORROW. THEY HAVEN'T VISITED SINCE EASTER.'

'I DIDN'T FORGET!' But she was making a face that said, 'Crap, I forgot.'

She pushed out her chair and moved to her bed. Before she jumped in, she scrolled through her music list, looking for something unlistenable, I imagine. Before she pressed play ...

'AOIFE, ARE YOU ASLEEP YET?'

She said nothing in response, instead waiting.

'GOOD!'

Aoife pressed play and closed her eyes. Since I was not here to watch other people sleep, I left the room and wandered downstairs. Her mother stood at the end of the stairs, looking up at Aoife's room. She looked annoyed.

'Thandi! Stop worrying. She's gone to sleep,' said a male voice from the living room. Aoife's father presumably.

'Why are you telling me to not worry? I can worry if I want to,' she responded. 'She always seems to be half asleep when people visit.'

Aoife's father walked out to the hall. From behind, he slid his hands around her waist and kissed her cheek.

'And you know my brother. He is always boasting about

how wonderful his daughter is, and mine looks like the living dead,' she said, her hand trembling.

'Don't worry,' he said, touching her hand. 'Aoife promised that she would wear her least-Goth clothes while he was here.'

She nodded. 'I wish the whole Christmas thing didn't go on for so long.'

A tear ran down her face, as if by accident. He brushed it away.

'Did you get the presents?' she asked.

'It's all taken care of.'

'Alex, thank you. I feel terrible that everyone has to cover for me. No wonder Aoife is the way she is …'

'It's okay. Aoife is fine and we don't mind. All we want is a nice calm Christmas, and also for your brother to not mention his daughter's college grades more than five times.'

She laughed and then they stood with each other in silence for a moment. I felt uncomfortable in a way I never had before. They were holding each other but it wasn't sexy; it was like they were supporting each other. An unnamed feeling caught hold of me and I walked away.

THIRTY-FOUR

So I didn't get any dirt on Aoife, but I did get an idea. I could only assume that her mother's mental health issues were very tiring for Aoife and her family. Did Aoife really need two people in her life like that? If I broke them up I'd be doing her a favour.

So I decided that the best thing would be to push Adam back down the road to self-loathing and depression, so that he would be intolerable to hang out with and Aoife would give up on their relationship. Presumably, once this happened, he would also lose his new group of friends. After all, they had been Aoife's friends first.

Unfortunately Adam was in a good place at that moment. His grades were steadily improving, people in school liked him more (well, 'like' is a strong word; we'll say 'regarded him as less of a freak' other than the odd trolling note) and he had a group of understanding friends and the key pillar of strength, Aoife. Thanks to their regular romantic entanglements that they appeared to mutually enjoy, his self-esteem was at its highest since I had known him (although that, to be fair, only covered the bones of six months). But I figured that if I chipped away at the foundations of this newfound confidence, and separated him from those who gave it to him, in time I could cause the whole thing to collapse. I just had to wait for an opportune time to make my first strike.

As it turned out, I didn't have to wait long. The week before Christmas Day they had a cinema date.

'Ten minutes late. Clearly someone doesn't value your time,' I said as we waited outside, 'leaving you to wait outside in the cold ...'

'I'm sure she has an explanation. Besides it's only ten minutes,' he said, his breath floating white in the air. 'Look, there she is.'

Blast, I thought, as I saw her running down the street.

'Sorry I'm late. My dad got into a fender bender when driving me here and there was this big argument and–'

'Is your dad okay?'

'No worries. He's fine!'

They kissed and then looked at the poster on the wall with all the movie times on it.

'Crap, we're too late for *Echo Chamber,*' said Aoife.

'Well, I guess that means we'll have to go see *The Golden Sword* instead,' said Adam.

What a coincidence! I bet that was the film she wanted to see, I was about to say.

'Yes, my cunning plan to see the film I want to see worked!' she said.

Damn! She *was* a cunning one. They queued up.

'Oh, you know what? Do you want to see *Santa Claus vs. Krampus* instead? It's on at the same time. It's about Santa Claus fighting a German Christmas devil.'

'Indecisive,' I said, tutting.

'Yes, we should go to that,' he said pointedly. I got the message.

I then proceeded to point out to Adam how flirty she was with the guy at the till, placing the €20 carefully into his hand and giving him a big, friendly smile. Adam gave me a withering look. Okay, it's possible I overstated how erotic the exchange of cash and tickets was.

Aoife handed Adam his ticket with a smile that suggested that my plan was never going to work. 'This sounds terrifying!'

'Terrifyingly bad, I bet. Time to see Kris Kringle kick some ass!'

They went to screen 3, passing the poster for *The Golden Sword*. There were loads of them all over the cinema. It showed a golden figure holding aloft a sword, with wizards cowering in fear. At least I didn't have to sit through that, I thought, but then I spied something with my little eye – a box in the corner of the poster that said, 'Warning: contains a graphic depiction of suicide.'

Oh, so that's why she suddenly changed her mind. She must have noticed the sign on the poster by the ticket box and decided to avoid it. With glee, I whispered in Adam's ear before they entered the dark room and pointed out the words on the poster. 'She clearly doesn't have a lot of faith in you, if she thinks you can't handle seeing something like that when it's just a silly movie.'

I could see from his face that I'd scored a bullseye.

THIRTY-FIVE

It was two days before Christmas Day (which judging by the decorations, constant songs and people running around with bags was a big deal) and a collection of old men and their grandsons were sailing tiny boats on the Lough. The models had little bits of tinsel on them and the humans wore red hats with fluffy white balls at the end. This must be a lovely moment for them, sharing what will undoubtedly one day be a treasured memory for both. Perhaps years from now one of the grandsons will be a rich man and own a yacht, one the same shade of red as his beloved grandaddy's little ship. That future sailor will take his own grandson by the shoulder and tell him of his grandfather and this beautiful moment.

Joy.

'That's very cute,' said Aoife, as they passed by.

'Why do we go on so many walks?' said Adam. They didn't really go on many walks, but I had been suggesting since the cinema that they go on a concerning amount.

Aoife turned her attention from a duck who was having a race with a water hen. 'What? Because we like walking? Or I do, anyway.'

'I just feel like we've been doing a lot of walking recently,' Adam said.

'Well, we can't drive and you don't have a bike.'

'That's true.'

Aoife looked at Adam funny and then looked back at the water, which at that moment was grey. 'Look at that swan. It looks like it could break your arm with its mind.'

'Oh, changing the subject …' I said, pouring further poison in his ear.

'Is it because they say depressed people should go for walks?'

'No … I just like walks. They are good for you,' said Aoife, who at this point was quite confused.

'You should remember this,' I told him. 'This is good for you, like you're some kind of dog that needs some exercise after being cooped up all day on its own.'

'So I'm like a dog that needs to be taken for walks.'

'I meant they are good for people in general, not you specifically,' said Aoife. 'Where is this coming from?'

'I just thought …'

'Go on, ask her about the cinema,' I said.

But, annoyingly, he said instead, 'Sorry, I'm being ridiculous. Stress of the holidays and all that.'

'Don't worry, I get it, being cooped up at home with my family, including my uncle. He's really intense and he keeps going on about his daughter. So getting out on a walk with you is actually a big relief for me.'

Oh, she was a clever one, twisting the argument around like that. This might be harder than I thought.

They stopped. In the centre of the Lough was a miniature house, with a man and a woman in long, flowing clothes, some animals and an empty bed made of hay. This had something to do with Christmas too.

Suddenly Aoife was holding a wrapped object in her hands. 'Open it now.'

'It's not Christmas yet,' he said, taking it.

'Yeah, but I'm not going to see you.'

'Shock, is this a book?'

He carefully opened it, peeling the tape off and folding the paper back. Slowly it revealed a picture of a boy with a scar on his forehead, standing in front of a red train.

I tried again. 'Typical,' I said, 'forcing her tastes on you.'

'This is great, I haven't read it!'

'I know. The best thing is if you like it – and you will – there are loads more in the series, so I have gifts sorted for the next few years.'

'Thank you,' he said, and gave her a kiss. A moment passed.

'Cough,' she said.

'I got you a gift too,' he said, passing her an envelope.

'Oh! You didn't need to,' she said, 'I always wanted … bus tickets to Dublin?'

'But wait, there's more,' he said, passing her a second, smaller envelope. Her eyes almost exploded when she saw the tickets.

'How did you know? They must be touring the new album. THANK YOU, THANK YOU, THANK YOU!'

Adam was now on the receiving end of a battery of kisses and they continued their walk around the Lough holding hands.

Bleurgh.

THIRTY-SIX

Christmas Day arrived and everything just stopped. No town, no work, no nothing; just sitting around watching movies, eating and drinking with a brief pause in the afternoon to exchange gifts. Adam got a PlayStation. He seemed happy about it.

I pointed out to Adam that he didn't give me a gift.

'Well, first of all, what do you get for the man who can't physically own anything, and secondly, you didn't get me one.'

'Well … I … shut up.'

It was a weird day, though I did enjoy the isolation from the rest of the world (although his mobile was still constantly beeping with little updates on Christmas in his girlfriend's house).

BIG NEWS! BARRY CAME OUT TO HIS
PARENTS – and they were totally cool with it!

Amazing!

'Oh, there's the phone again. I wonder who that could be,' his dad said, winking, before taking another sip of wine. (The precautionary ban on alcohol in the house had been temporarily lifted for Christmas. Since Adam was doing so well, why not celebrate it?)

He was in a very jovial mood ('jovial' being today's term in the 'Word of the Day' calendar Adam gave his mum). After watching a movie about a guy singing songs while jumping in puddles, everyone sat down to eat dinner and my word it was massive. Plate after plate of food, meat and various things made of potato. After massacring the dishes, they sat back.

'We should give thanks,' said Dad, his paper crown slightly atilt.

'That's a very American suggestion,' said Mum.

'Fine, a toast so,' he said, raising a glass. 'I just wanted to say that it has been a challenging year for this family, but here we are at Christmas, all of us together, safe and sound.'

'Hear, hear,' said Mum, also a little tipsy.

'I'm thankful that, after his scare, Adam is doing really well. Friends, doing well in school, even a girlfriend. You've done it, kid.'

Adam was blushing. He wasn't enjoying this attention.

'Um, okay, Dad. Thanks for all your help.'

I watched this all with a certain amount of glee. While I was undermining his confidence by turning him against his girlfriend, now his father was unintentionally helping me out by dragging up the bad memories of what happened earlier in the year, reminding Adam of who he had been. I was sure I could use this.

'I'm not going to lie. We were worried, very worried. Like when we came back and …' Dad trailed to an uncomfortable stop.

'I think you've said enough, dear,' said Mum.

'Yes, sorry, forgetting myself. Anyway, Merry Christmas. May we all be together again next year.'

When the family settled down to watch *EastEnders* with trifle, I whispered in Adam's ear: 'You'd better be careful not to let them down again. Seems like they don't want to have to deal with another incident. You'd better be a happy chappy from now on. But hey, no pressure.'

Although he didn't look at me when I said this, I could see his whole body tense. Turns out I got a gift for Christmas after all.

THIRTY-SEVEN

Linda said that we shouldn't be here and she was probably right.

'Linda, it's okay. No one is going to see us,' said Aoife.

'I'm not worried about that. I'm worried about this thing falling apart.'

Cork is an old city with a fair few ancient buildings. Many are dilapidated rotting piles of brick and stone and are one strong wind away from collapsing onto any passers-by. Long abandoned, these death traps are completely uninhabitable and therefore perfect for the first post-Christmas hangout.

The particular house we were gathered in was a two-storey house that was missing its second floor, at least most of it. All that remained were the stairs leading up and a small segment of floor that was wide enough for four people to sit on, although I can't say if it was strong enough to hold them. I would have guessed not, since every move they made elicited a groan of timbers.

'The smell …' said Linda.

'It reminds me of Barry,' said Douglas.

'Where is Barry?' said Aoife.

'He's bringing Andrew to meet his parents,' said Linda.

'So hanging out in the epitome of urban decay with his friends is no longer good enough for him,' said Douglas with a hint of a smile.

'Oh, give over, Douglas,' said Aoife. 'How was your Christmas?'

'Terrible. It all started on Christmas Eve. Father insisted that I play piano accompaniment in the local church …'

As Douglas described his holiday in vivid detail, Adam remained quiet. He sat against the wall, next to Aoife. I had spent the last few days trying to convince him that he was going to let his parents down, that he was damaging their mental health having to worry about him all the time, that the stress on their marriage of having a mentally unstable teenager might be too much and I wouldn't be surprised if it ruined his relationship with Aoife (I was over-egging it a bit to be fair), so he made a point of sitting next to her. It's amazing how insidious a suggestion can be. Once he got the idea in his head, it just grew and grew. It put an edge on things. He hadn't mentioned it to Aoife, though, as I reminded him that the last thing she needed in her life was another problem person that she would have to spend her time looking after. But it was definitely noticeable. Out of earshot of Adam, Linda had already asked Aoife if he was all right.

Aoife put her hand in Adam's and it tightened.

Linda shifted her body into a more comfortable position as gently as possible, which meant the floor only vibrated a frightening amount rather than a terrifying amount. 'So is it this weekend you're heading to Dublin?'

'No, next weekend. It should be fun.'

Douglas looked at them and smirked. 'Well, with Captain

Chatty here, it's sure to be a blast.'

Adam let go of her hand. Good.

'Douglas …' said Aoife. I immediately told Adam that she was going to defend him because that was something she felt she had to do. And I reminded him how he didn't do that for her at the gig.

Adam abruptly stood up. The wood moaned. 'I'm going to go.'

Douglas rolled his eyes. 'It was a joke. Don't be so sensitive.'

Adam stepped forward and in two paces was standing at the edge of the remaining floorboards. He stared down at the underneath mess of mangled furniture and manky wood. This pit was once someone's life.

'Jesus, Adam. What are you doing?' said Linda, grabbing him and pulling him back.

'Nothing. Sorry. I'm in a weird mood. Actually I do have to go. My mum's collecting me.'

Aoife said, 'It's probably best we all go. I don't trust these floorboards any more.'

'Huzzah,' Douglas said, 'I've ruined everything.'

Geez, give me some credit.

They walked down one by one. Once everyone was out the door, I thought I heard a crash inside, but no one else seemed to notice.

THIRTY-EIGHT

The applause died down as the musician left the stage. Adam wasn't clapping; instead he was sitting in a sullen silence beside the aisle, in case he needed to escape, I guess.

The principal cleared his throat. 'Up next, we have Lorcán, a survivor of depression and a suicide attempt. I'm sure he'll have many great insights to share with us on today's topic.'

There was a smattering of applause as Lorcán stepped up to the podium.

The lights must have been warm in the auditorium, because Adam was sweating an unusual amount. His entire year was in the room, fifth and sixth too. 'Thank you, Mr O'Neill,' said the speaker, a man in his thirties but wearing a Ramones T-shirt and jeans. 'Hey guys, I know what you are thinking. "It's another guy talking about Mental Health and mindfulness and yada yada yada."'

Adam stopped paying attention and his hand entered his trouser pocket. He pulled out his phone, looking for a distraction I suspect. As the screen lit up, there was a cough from the principal and a glare at Adam.

'When I was your age I was suffering, but I didn't have a name for my illness. It was a vague sadness that grew and grew. Today I am going to give you the name of it – depression. Now you may scoff, but once you can name the enemy, you can fight it, deal with its underhanded schemes.'

Adam glanced at me. I felt the sudden desire to defend myself but I couldn't think of anything to say. It suddenly seemed very claustrophobic in the hall. I needed to get out.

'Should we get out of here?' I suggested. 'I … you look stressed.'

Adam turned to see if he could find Miss Campbell, but before he could get her attention something happened.

'Excuse me, I have a question!' said someone, interrupting the speaker, his hand in the air.

'There will be time for questions at the end,' said the principal.

But Lorcán said, 'One couldn't hurt. What is it?'

Philip stood up, making it clear it was him asking the question. 'Why would someone hit themselves in the head with a hammer?'

This was an interesting development.

'Excuse me?'

'Wouldn't you say that you would have to be an idiot to try and kill yourself with a hammer?'

'Philip,' said the principal, 'sit down, right now.'

Adam stood up. 'Shouldn't you be asking me, Philip?'

The teachers standing at the back of the hall had a look of horror on their faces. I think I heard one say, 'Stop filming.'

'The truth is I wanted to,' Adam said. 'Why? I don't know. Because I'm a terrible person? Because life was crap?'

Philip smirked.

'Lads, I don't think this is quite the time–' began Lorcán,

who had not anticipated this.

'I have another question,' Philip persevered. 'How come you managed to survive, while my brother, a person people actually liked, died?'

'Well, I didn't have the motivation that having you as a brother would have given me to succeed,' said Adam.

The audience gasped, except for one guy in the corner whose applause was enthusiastic. Even Adam seemed momentarily shocked by what he had said. Time froze, perhaps in the hope it could reverse itself and correct this mistake, but the freeze was broken by a scream of 'I'M GOING TO KILL YOU!'

Philip launched himself from his seat, but tripped over the student next to him and fell on his face. Relieved laughter exploded.

'Philip Hurly! Go to my office right now!' shouted the principal. 'This is disgraceful behaviour.'

The speaker stood in the middle of the stage, not sure how to continue.

In a sulk, Philip got up and walked up the aisle, glaring daggers at Adam. Miss Campbell took Adam by the arm. 'It's probably best you come with me.'

Retreating to an empty classroom, Miss Campbell sat him down, then leaned against the teacher's desk.

'I'm sorry, Miss.'

'Adam, you're not in trouble. Philip was clearly trying to antagonise you. Granted, that probably wasn't the best response, but–'

'I don't know why he hates me.'

'Philip doesn't hate you. He's just in a lot of pain over his brother and needs someone to blame.'

'So it *is* my fault?'

'No, no. No one is to blame. What Chris did was … well, who knows what he was thinking when he did what he did. Adam, I want you to know that you're not an idiot and you're not a terrible human being. You are a worthwhile human being. And you're a good writer.'

Adam nodded a tired, hollow nod, then began to cry. A huge flood of tears. They continued until he ran out of them, just in time for his parents' arrival. They wore a familiar expression, though one I had not seen in a while. But it was good to see it – it meant I was another step closer to getting the old Adam back.

THIRTY-NINE

'STAND CLEAR, LUGGAGE DOOR OPERATING,' the bus said with an air of menace unusual for public transport. The side of the Cork to Dublin bus opened to take any large bags, but Aoife and Adam didn't need it as they had all their stuff in a backpack. They got on and Adam took the window seat. The day was completely planned. They would get up to Dublin round oneish, have some lunch, wander around the National Gallery and then see the band at seven that evening. After that, they would stay with one of Aoife's aunts.

Aoife made some effort to make conversation, but Adam was unresponsive, preferring to stare out the window. His weekend was being pre-emptively soured by his mood. Also I kept reminding him how embarrassing the whole school thing was.

'Have you been to Dublin before?'

'Mmm.'

'I've only been there once before.'

He said nothing in response. This was perfect.

'I can't wait to go to the National Gallery.'

'Yip.'

'I think I'll just talk to myself for the whole three-hour bus ride.'

'Mmm.'

'Super.'

Aoife pulled out her headphones and turned up the volume to ear-damaging levels. Adam pretended not to notice this and watched more fields pass by. It took three hours to get to Dublin from Cork and they felt every minute of it.

Finally, after they arrived in Dublin and were sitting in a café having a late lunch, Aoife asked him the question.

'Adam, is something wrong?' She clearly knew the answer to this.

'No,' he said predictably, before pouring too much milk into his tea. 'Crap.'

'Are you sure?'

His hand shook. 'I'm fine.'

'She knows you are lying. She's worried about you,' I whispered in his ear.

'So do you still want to go see Cannibal Corpse? We don't have to if you don't want to. We could head straight to my aunt's or go to the cinema or something.'

'She thinks you are a problem that needs to be fixed.'

'Why would you ask that?' Adam said, not responding to me.

'I just want to make sure you are okay.'

'Aoife, why are you going out with me?'

There is a high chance I imagined this, but I'm positive that everything in the world ground to a halt when he said this. Aoife, surprised, took a second to respond. 'I like you? I dunno, the usual reasons. Why are you asking me?'

'I'm not an idiot. I'm not someone who needs charity.'

'What the hell, Adam? What's that supposed to mean?'

'Fine. We won't talk about it.'

'Fine.'

Aoife bit into her bourbon biscuit, angrily. 'Actually, it's not fine. What exactly is your problem?' she said.

'Why? Do you want to solve it? Make me your special little project?'

'I have no idea what you are on about.'

'You and your depressed boyfriend. It makes you feel good, does it?'

'Adam, stop this.'

'Tell her, Adam.'

'I know why you are dating me. You want to solve my problems. You think you can save me from my demons, make me better, a normal human being. You want to help me, just because you can't help your mother ...'

Adam trailed off when he saw that his words had hit home. Aoife's eyes widened and she opened her mouth to reply but then said nothing.

'It's true, isn't it?'

'Adam, I don't know what has happened or what I said, but I'm leaving and I don't want to talk to you. I really like you, you are not a charity case, not someone for me to fix, but I can't be around you right now.'

'Wait–'

'PISS OFF, ADAM,' she shouted with tears welling, but resisting crying in his presence. 'Just leave me alone.'

She stood up and grabbed her things. In her frustration, she tipped the rucksack over and her scarf rolled onto the floor. Everyone was watching. A tear fell as she walked out.

A waitress approached the table. 'Are you okay?'

'Sorry.'

'Honestly, take your time. I remember how bad break-ups can be.'

'I don't think it was … I'm just going to go.' He looked through his wallet and discovered he only had coins on him. It took an agonisingly long time for him to count out the correct change.

Finally it was just me and Adam again. Although it didn't quite satisfy me as much as I had hoped. Surely I wasn't feeling guilty?

As we left the café Adam looked at me. 'I should go and find her, shouldn't I? I'm such a jerk. Why did I say those things?'

So we weren't out of the woods yet.

'No, Aoife was at fault here. She shouldn't be trying to fix you, she should accept you for who you are, and you called her on it. If anything, you need to get away from her.'

As we boarded the next bus to Cork, Adam's phone rang over and over again, and it didn't stop ringing until we were about an hour out of town. She sent text messages too, but on my advice, Adam didn't read them. It would only make things worse. Perversely he didn't turn off his phone, preferring to hear every disappointment in his pocket. Eventually it stopped and only then did he pull his phone out, and some pieces of paper fell out along with it.

He had the concert tickets … and her bus ticket home too.

That's probably why she was calling, I told him, it wasn't because she actually cared about him.

He glared at the back of the bus seat in front of him. The bus was nearly empty, presumably because people generally have better things to do on a Saturday afternoon than take the five o'clock Dublin to Cork bus. Things which don't include stranding your girlfriend in the middle of an unfamiliar city.

'It's okay. You still have me,' I said.

He began to cry, quite loudly in fact.

Oh.

I had a bad feeling about this.

IV

HEY, THAT'S NO WAY
TO SAY GOODBYE

FORTY

'How are you feeling today?' said Dr Moore.

'I'm okay,' Adam said. 'It was pretty rough there for a while, but I think things are going better.'

Well, Adam was lying, things had gotten significantly worse. A month had passed since the big break-up and the only thing that had gotten better was his ability to pretend that everything was peachy.

'How do you feel about the school incident now?'

'Philip is going through his own stuff and, while it wasn't nice to hear, I realise now that he was taking out his anger about what happened to his brother on me and that really it had nothing to do with me.'

He was telling Dr Moore exactly what he wanted to hear.

'I'm happy to hear you can take such a positive view on this.'

Oh, Adam was getting good at this.

'And Aoife?'

***

'Hey, guys,' Adam said, 'I'm heading out to meet the lads.'

'Have fun!' said Mum.

Adam loudly closed the front door, but rather than head for town, he turned and crept along the side of the house. Waiting until his mother was safely out of the kitchen, the windows of which overlooked the back garden, he went to the shed. There was not much risk of being caught in there, since his dad's gardening inclinations went into hibernation during winter.

He took out his phone, plugged the charger into the workbench and started to watch TV. This he did for five hours.

When it started to get dark, he cautiously emerged from the shed and returned to the house via the front door.

'Hey, Adam, how was town?' said his mum.

'Good,' he said.

'Did you see Aoife?' she said hopefully.

'Oh, she started debating in school. Takes up loads of time, so the gang is not seeing that much of her.'

Since the trip to Dublin, he had seen her precisely once. It was in the distance on the way home from Dr Moore's office. He hid behind a tree.

'Well, here's your dinner,' Mum said.

It was bizarre watching him, like watching a familiar movie with the wrong language. He was bright and sunny to such an unusual degree that I'm surprised no one around him realised it was all an act. But I guess it was easy for me to see through, since I saw the other side so much.

After dinner, he slipped up to his room and lay in silence for several hours, just me and him. I was so bored I had to keep reminding myself that this was what I had wanted.

'Want to do some writing?' I said, to try to stir him into work.

He shook his head.

There was a single knock on the door.

Traditionally, Dad knocked three times and opened it when there was no answer. (The lock had long since been removed.) Adam waited, and when nothing happened he heaved himself up and opened the door. It was Douglas.

'Ah … hi.'

'What's the deal, Adam?'

'What do you mean?'

'Where the hell are you? You've gotten very good at coming to Dr Moore's just too late to run into me.'

'I'm embarrassed. Over that whole Aoife thing. She's probably still really angry.'

'Dude, she's worried about you … and, yes, a little angry. You did ditch her in *Dublin*,' said Douglas, the name of the capital city spoken with such disdain it suggested that there was an interesting story there.

'Well, tell her I'm fine. That way she can go back to being angry at me.'

'You're not fine. Despite what you've apparently been telling your mum.'

'You didn't tell her, did you?'

'No, although I should have. I had to come up with a story, on the spot, about what we did in town today. You're lucky I'm such a master of spinning yarns.'

Adam was relieved. 'You know, I'm just having a break. Also, who made you the master of sanity?'

Douglas exhaled slightly, as if resisting saying something regrettable, and pulled a card out of his breast pocket and handed it to Adam. It looked like it came from a board game. Adam turned it upside down and recognised it from the Monopoly game. 'I'm giving you a "Get Out of Jail Free" card. I realise you are going through a shitty time, where everything is stale and hateful, but we are here. Even though you are being a complete dick, we like you and don't want you to off yourself, so here is a reminder that you can return to Paul Street any time.'

Adam stood there, looking at Douglas. I could see in his eyes that he wanted nothing more than to have things go back to the way they were before. I wanted to tell him to take the card, to use it, to go back to normality, but that would mean admitting I was wrong.

'That first time, when you invited me to join you in the car park. Why did you do that?'

'You looked like you were having a bad time and it's easier to deal with a bad time with people around you.'

'So you felt sorry for me.'

Douglas rolled his eyes. 'That's not what I meant. The thing is, we are all weirdos. If we don't look out for each other, who will?'

'Thanks, Douglas,' said Adam. 'I might see you around.'

'If I don't see you in town next Monday after school, I'm telling Dr Moore and your parents.'

'Okay, okay. I'll be there.'

Adam watched from his window as Douglas walked outside and was joined by Barry at the front. Barry said something and Douglas shrugged. When they glanced up at his window, Adam ducked behind the curtains.

'He's friends with Barry again,' he said, 'probably because I'm not there.'

'That doesn't make sense.'

'I bet he only came because he wants to feel better in case something happens. Then at least he can say he made the effort.'

Adam was trapped in this horrible logic, which assumed the worst of everyone. All I had wanted was Adam all to myself but, now that I had him, I wasn't sure I wanted this Adam.

FORTY-ONE

On Monday Adam walked out through the school gates. School had become torturous since the incident at the mental health day – a definite coolness had developed towards him. Philip had been suspended for a week but upon his return had set about spinning what happened so that Adam was seen as the real bully in the situation. (How he did this must have been convincing, since most of the students now looked at Adam with mistrustful eyes.) He no longer raised his hand in class. His grades were slipping back. In class his notebooks were empty.

'Are we going to go to town?' I said.

He shook his head and we walked home.

'I think Douglas was bluffing,' said Adam.

We walked on in silence for a few minutes, Adam working on automatic. I had hoped things would eventually balance out and he would return to just getting by, but he seemed to be slipping deeper and deeper into his dark mood. In making my perfect plan, I had failed to consider the fact that I had only known him on the way up. This was the way down, and it was dark at the bottom.

'You know, maybe I will go–' he started to say, before we were rudely interrupted by a whopper of a punch to the back of his head. He fell to the ground, but recovered quickly enough to turn over and see that Philip and some of his friends had ambushed him.

Philip slammed his fist into Adam's stomach, decommissioning him completely. Schoolbags whacked into the side of his head, and fists piled on.

Philip, raising his fist again, said, 'It's your fault he's dead. You put the idea in his head.'

'Wha–'

Wham. A kick to the side.

Lying on the ground, Adam had one chance and he took it. He kicked out straight and true, catching Philip right in the balls. It was not the most dignified of manoeuvres but it was effective.

Philip fell to the ground and, while his friends were distracted, Adam jumped up and ran away as best as he could, although it was more of a stagger. He wasn't far from home and when he got there he went straight to the shed.

Using his phone camera, he surveyed the damage. His face was covered in red welts but there seemed to be no bruises. If he was smart enough, he could probably manage to stop his parents noticing. He looked in the window of the house – there was no one home yet. He snuck in the door and ran upstairs to his room.

He sent a text. 'Meeting Aoife after school! Hopefully making things up! No need to make me dinner.' Clearly his plan was to avoid them for the evening.

'No worries, have a fab time! xx,' replied his mother.

I guess Douglas hadn't told her yet.

He looked exhausted and tears were involuntarily making

their way down his cheeks. He set an alarm to wake himself up in a few hours (he would need to make an appearance before bedtime or else his parents would have questions). He lay back on his bed and fell into a deep but troubled sleep. Once he was out, I needed to leave. Music jangled somewhere in the city so I followed it. I didn't want to think about Adam any more.

Many of the shops had giant hearts in the windows and were advertising chocolates and flowers and romantic dinners. Outside one restaurant, I saw Miss Campbell waiting. I didn't recognise her immediately since she was dressed up. She lit up when she looked my way and for a moment I thought it was me she was smiling at. Then I realised the smile was for the man behind me. He approached and they gave each other a little kiss, then walked arm in arm to a nearby pub. Why did I think she saw me? Why did I hope she saw me? Why would anyone be happy to see me?

It was time I admitted it to myself. Adam was never going to be happy to see me. I had convinced myself that there was a magical period where everything was golden, but there wasn't. I had romanticised our shared gloom. That we had things in common and only needed each other. In reality I realised I was simply a reminder of a bad time, one he had been trying his best to learn to live with.

I found myself once again outside Philip's house. I admit, it wasn't purely out of nosiness I came here. The truth was I was always hoping to see Chris, a replay of the one time someone seemed happy to see me. I was suddenly seized with the idea that tonight was the night. I would find him.

I entered through his window first. Inside everything was still impeccably preserved. There was no hint of Philip's night-time sojourns.

'Chris!' I called. No response. I turned around and saw him floating by the door. I repeated his name but got no response. 'Chris!'

No response. I inched closer and, in a moment, felt defla-ted. It was just his school uniform hanging on the door. I felt a red rush of regret; this must be what embarrassment feels like.

I could hear noises from downstairs. Philip's mother was shouting at him. Someone must have told on him.

'Philip, what are we going to do with you? I hear about stuff like this and I worry I'm going to lose two sons!'

'I'm sorry. I just have … I don't know … I'm just so angry. Why did he do it?'

She hugged him, the two of them crying.

The radio was on in the next room. It was Adam's mother reading the news. Listening to it I could detect no sign that she had any clue of the torment her son was in. With an un-wavering voice, she read the bad news of the day. I remem-bered what she said about one day reporting Adam's death, and for a moment I thought I could hear it, carefully worded to avoid glamorisation: '*Another suicide was reported today in Cork city. The family asks for privacy in this difficult time.*'

That was it. Just because he didn't like me, that didn't mean he should be doomed. I was going to save him.

I thought myself quite noble at that moment. I returned home to await whatever tomorrow would bring.

FORTY-TWO

He woke up early and it was quite the transformation. Perhaps he had also had an epiphany in his sleep. It was like everything since Christmas had disappeared, rolled away overnight.

He put on his uniform, tying his tie perfectly. He walked downstairs and found his mother pulling shopping bags from a bigger bag. She looked tired. He smiled.

'Hey, Adam,' said Mum, 'you look cheerful this morning.'

'I'm not allowed to be in a good mood?' he said teasingly.

She stopped what she was doing and looked at him. 'Oh, of course,' she said. 'It's just recently … never mind. Are you ready for school?'

'I am.'

This was astounding. Perhaps a good sleep was all he needed.

She dropped him outside the gates of St Jude's. He whistled as he walked.

A moment later he asked, 'Is Mum still there?'

I looked behind me. The car was parked.

'Yeah. Why?'

'No worries,' he said, not answering my question, 'we can get around that.'

He walked through the front doors, passed through the crowd of students waiting for their classes to start, continued down the corridor, stepped through the emergency exit that everyone knew the alarm for was broken and, in less than five minutes, was once again outside.

'Aren't we going to class? It's English this morning.'

'No, I'm going to kill myself instead.'

He looked at his phone. He had no messages, but he turned it off anyway. He would need to ignore it for the day. It would become obvious soon enough that he was on the hop and they would call his parents.

'I don't think that's a good idea.'

'It just seems like the best thing for everyone. I've been thinking about it a lot recently and now I'm sure.'

'But why today? Why not next week? Tomorrow even?'

'I dunno. Today is just as good as any other.'

We were heading for town. We passed Grand Parade where the Christmas Ferris wheel had recently stood, but it looked now as if it had never been there. He stopped at a bus stop.

I was confused. We were getting the bus. The 220 to Ballincollig appeared and we got on. The driver looked at his grey trousers.

'Shouldn't you be in school?'

'I'm going home sick,' Adam offered as a flimsy excuse.

'Are we going to Aoife's?' I asked, as we sat in the back.

'Yip.'

'Won't she be in school?'

'Hopefully.'

Then it dawned on me. Adam needed some method of self-destruction. There was none in his house. His parents had made sure of that. But he knew where one was. The boxes of pills in Aoife's house.

One bus journey later, Adam was standing outside her door. He peered in the window to make sure no one was home. He picked up the pot next to the front door. The key was underneath.

'Lucky me.' Adam opened the door as slowly and quietly as possible, in case someone was home. But the house was quiet.

He crept up the stairs.

He found the bathroom.

He opened the cabinet.

A sound interrupted him. Someone *was* in the house!

Adam grabbed a couple of boxes of pills and slipped them into his school bag.

The sound again. It was a snore. It was coming from Aoife's room.

Adam peeked through her bedroom door, which was a little ajar, and so did I. Aoife was in bed, surrounded by tissues and brown bottles. Adam looked worried.

'She must have the flu,' he whispered.

'You'll have the flu and a prison sentence for breaking and entering if you hang out here much longer,' I said.

Adam paused for a moment and then whispered something. As if somehow hearing it, she stirred, murmured in her sleep, but didn't wake.

'Alright, let's go.'

Then, from downstairs, came the sound of the front door opening. Aoife's mother came in holding a bag of groceries, most likely filled with healthy things to help her ailing daughter, and humming the Healy's Bread jingle. As her hands were full she left the door open. When she walked into the kitchen, we crept out as quietly as possible.

'Goodbye, Aoife,' Adam said sadly as he walked away. 'You're better off without a boyfriend who breaks your heart and breaks into your house.'

I felt a rush of guilt. I had blamed her. To me, she was the one who ruined things. Everything would have been fine if she hadn't complicated things. But that wasn't really her fault. If it was anyone's fault … I dismissed that thought.

We took the bus back into town and I tried to convince him to change his mind.

'This is not a good idea. You shouldn't do this.'

'You're just worried about what will happen to you.'

Actually I hadn't thought of that. What would happen to me? Would I wander the Earth? Would I go to Heaven (or the other place)? Maybe I would just disappear. I didn't want to find out the answer.

'Think of all the people who will miss you.'

'It will be hard for them at first, but in the long run, they'll be glad to be rid of the burden.'

'But what about you? You'll miss out on so much!'

He paused and looked straight at me. 'You don't understand. I can't deal with things any more. No one likes me in school, I stuffed up everything with Aoife, Mum and Dad are constantly worried. Everything is just broken.'

The bus arrived in town and we disembarked.

'Adam!' called a voice.

Adam turned and saw it was Linda, who was carrying something in a large box, being directed by her mother.

'Hey, Linda.'

'Are you on the hop?'

'Ah yeah, I guess.'

'Nice. Just a second, Mum. I'm on the way to the dentist. Look, I know you were a dick to Aoife, but we are still around and we're worried about you. Come back to Paul Street!'

'Oh, yeah, I was going through a rough patch but I'll see you on Saturday,' said Adam, making a promise he had no intention of keeping. 'Oh and tell Aoife to get well soon!'

'Sure?' said Linda, waving him off.

***

This was it. Here we were. It was surreal.

I thought he would try to take them all at once. His parents could come home looking for him at any minute, so time was of the essence. But, no, instead he took one at a time. If he was going to do it, I kind of just wanted it over and done with. At one point he did speed up, but ended up coughing up a few in his impatience, nearly choking himself (which is funny if you think about it).

I made one last try to dissuade him. 'I don't understand. How did it get so bad so quickly? You seemed happy enough at Christmas.'

He looked at me.

'It's always bad. Even when things were okay, they were still bad. I was able to ignore it for a while, but it's always been bubbling underneath, waiting to overwhelm me.'

'Did you write a note?' I asked. He grabbed a page, scribbled something on it and left it lying on the desk with a book on the corner to prevent it from getting lost.

'Let's see what your final words are.'

In large print in blue biro it said: SORRY.

Sorry. Sorry with a full stop. I couldn't process this. Where was the purple prose? Where was the explanation? Where was the heartfelt missive to his loved ones?

I looked at him. He looked sorry. I couldn't understand. Why was he sorry? Philip drove him to it with his bullying and blame, Aoife drove him to it with her selfishness, his parents drove him to it with their lack of understanding.

He was sitting there.

'Why are you saying sorry?'

'It's my fault.'

'How is it your fault?'

'I dunno. My general existence.'

'You idiot, this isn't your fault. It's mine.'

The final words fell hard in my mind, a revelation. I had been blaming him and Aoife for my unhappiness. But it wasn't his fault or hers. He was a sad boy who got stuck with a dick of a ghost who couldn't stand the idea of someone else being happy. I looked at Adam. He was beginning to wobble. I realised that we didn't have much time left.

'Adam!'

'Mmmmph.'

'Adam, we need to ring the hospital.'

'What?'

'There is still time to stop this. I just need you to ring someone.'

Adam looked at me funny.

'I … I need to stop this.'

I'd been wrong. Why didn't I realise this earlier? It wasn't fair. I should be able to change my mind. More than anything, I wanted to stop this but I had nothing. All I could do was talk. Talk, talk, talk. *If only I could grab him*, I thought.

I reached out my hand and grabbed his arm.

It stopped.

He looked at this, shocked. He dropped the remainder of the pills on the floor. There were a lot left. He really had only taken a few, at least that was what I hoped.

'We can be okay,' I said but I couldn't hear myself. Everything was getting woozy. I guessed this was sleep at last.

The landline rang somewhere in the white.

And then we faded away.

EPILOGUE
THE FUTURE

ONE

I ran into him on North Main Street. It was a morning in April, technically spring but it still felt like winter. I had debated what the ideal form for our meeting was. My decided plan was to write him a very well-thought-out email that would spare us the embarrassment of a meeting in school (and the possibility of me being punched in the head again).

However, when I saw him leave GameMania, he was on his own, staring at the game he had just bought. The sun struck in just the right way and I decided that the moment was perfect. If I didn't do it right now, I would never do it.

'Hey!' I shouted, running down the street.

'What do you want?' he growled. He literally growled at me, like a bear. If I didn't make my follow-up statement amazing, there would be a good chance of decapitation.

'I … You probably don't want to hear this or anything, but I think it's important for me to say two things. Number 1, Philip, I'm sorry your brother died and for what I said at the talk that day. I was going through a bad time. No, actually, no excuses. It was completely out of line.'

He seemed genuinely surprised by this breathless condolence. I was unclear if this was a good thing or bad, so I continued anyway, as what I had to say was not going to get any better.

'Number 2. It's not my fault. I'm not sure what Chris was

going through, but what he did, he was going to do because of him and not because of me. He didn't see me and think "Hey! Adam is a cool dude. I should try that." I do realise this may not be the most appropriate thing to say to a grieving person, but you have made my life more crappy than it needs to be and I would prefer if you stopped. I'm not asking to be friends or anything and I'm not blaming you for what happened after Christmas, but please, when you see me in the future, just ignore me.'

Philip stood there. I could not tell what his reaction was. I tensed my leg muscles in case I had to run away. But after a few moments he nodded.

'Can I ask you a question, Adam?' he said.

'Sure.'

'When you did try to kill yourself, with the hammer or the other time, why did you do it?'

'Do you really want to know?'

'Yes, I want to understand.'

I had not expected this development.

'Well, it might take a while.'

'I'm free now if you are.'

'I guess.'

We spent the next three-quarters of an hour sitting upstairs in Marks and Spencer's café, just having a chat. He apologised for the fight (apparently Chris's inquest was later that week and he wasn't handling it very well at the time) and I just talked about me and my problems out loud. We parted not as friends or enemies, but as two guys from the same class who'd both had a bad year.

***

Here are things I have learned recently.

Overdosing on pills has a surprisingly low success rate for suicide.

Having your stomach pumped is an extremely unpleasant experience.

Learning the previous two things puts a damper on your day.

Something seemed different after the second attempt. I'm not sure what, although starting on medication probably helped. There was no question of me not taking pills after my second attempt. My parents made me take them in front of them for the first two months (and still check if my supplies are depleting at the correct rate).

Still, even after everything, I'll admit I was scared of the effect they might have. While I didn't like me, I didn't want to change me, lose any important part of me. I worried I wouldn't be able to write any more, that the part of me that distinguished me from everyone else in a room would fade away, vanish in a plume of smoke.

After two weeks on the medication, I sat down, paper on the desk, pen ready for action (the first week on the pills was rough, but things smoothed out somewhat after that). I put the tip to the page and, after a moment's hesitation, I began to write. I wrote for three pages, a story about a hungry kid on the street chasing a rat so he would have something to eat. I was still worried about things. The stuff I wrote was still grim and depressing. I was still me. So I remained the same, except everything felt more even.

Going back to the day I ambushed Philip, that evening I walked with Aoife along the river, headed towards the Observatory. The occasion was the exciting comeback/second gig of The Laypersons, with the trio together again at last – Douglas, Barry and Sinead. The reason for the reunion of the original crew depended on who you asked. Barry said that The Laypersons couldn't survive without his precision drumming. Douglas said Barry's playing was cheaper than buying batteries for the drum machine. I don't really know what Sinead said since I don't know her very well, but we have hung out a few times since then and she seems cool.

Aoife and I are still somehow friends, but we agreed that our relationship was probably not a good idea, at least until we both figured ourselves out. She is still amazing, though, smart and pretty and all those things. I thought of that as we got closer to the large telescope which pointed skyward. It was a bit of a walk from the city centre so we had lots of time to talk about what we were writing at the moment, the new haircut of Fintan from our writing group and whether I should get the same haircut to confuse people.

The stage was still being set up as we arrived. We could

see Linda and Andrew waiting in the crowd. The band were tuning up.

'Soundcheck guy, can you please check our sound?' said Douglas.

They hadn't seen us yet, so before we joined them we gazed up at the stars poking through the sheet of space. It was infinite, which, to be honest, I don't really understand, so instead I thought of it as really deep, a well with no visible bottom, with dots of light reflecting.

'At last, I've shown you some real stars,' I said.

Aoife laughed. 'Man, you would be a great boyfriend if you weren't such a terrible boyfriend.'

'That's fair.'

We sat on the grass, our hands tantalisingly close. For now, the dew on the grass would have to do. I really owe Aoife so much. What happened was that when I told Linda to tell her to get well soon, I hadn't realised that no one knew she was sick, since it had just come on that morning. Linda texted Aoife to find out what was going on and Aoife, who had been woken up by her mother at this point, realised the only way I could have known was if I had been in the house. She put two and two together and saw that the bathroom pills were gone. Then she rang my phone and when she saw it was off, she rang the radio station my mum worked at. Fearing the worst, Mum raced home, ringing the landline as she drove, and found me.

I owe Aoife so much that the least I could do was not try to get her to go out with me again.

I do owe one other person, although it was also kind of his fault, so only partial credit. When I woke up in the hospital, my stomach in bits and my head a mess, the room was filled by my parents and doctors, but he was there too, standing in the corner. He was, as usual, pale as a sheet, with eyes which looked permanently forlorn. After all this time, he had the exact same appearance, a monochrome copy of me the night I died: his face and T-shirt covered with blood, one shoelace permanently untied for eternity. It's strange, he looked like me but in the way a painting looks like its subject, somehow both vivid and flat. I remember the first time I saw him I was so frightened, but this time he was the one who looked scared.

'Hey you,' I said and he smiled.

Sometime later, at night, when we were alone, he told me he had a theory about why he was able to move around at night when I was asleep. He partly realised it the night Aoife and I had ... you know, but finally figured it out later. If I wasn't thinking of him, he was no longer tied to me. That was the first night I completely let him go.

'That's it?'

'That's it.'

'You sure?

'Well, we have to test it.'

'Okay. How?'

'I guess you should try to forget me.'

It's hard to forget your own ghost, you know, but he tried his best to help. For the next month, he stayed quiet and out of sight, hiding behind my back, although I always knew he was there. I thought this was silly.

However, one Friday, Aoife and Douglas and co. visited and I was so delighted that I completely forgot about him. When they left, I suddenly remembered and, poof, he appeared in front of me.

'Where did you go?'

'Oh, just down the road. Snooped in the shop.'

'That's pretty anticlimactic.'

He laughed.

So that was it. Sometimes I see him and sometimes I don't think of him.

That evening I sat under a purple sky watching the band tune up. I could see him, he was still here, my ghost. I thought about everything that had happened during the past year. Then, a second later, Aoife's fingers touched mine and didn't move away, so now I'm smiling at nothing because I'm still here.

ACKNOWLEDGEMENTS

I have the odd habit of checking the acknowledgements at the back first when starting a book, so I can't tell you how excited I am to finally write my own. Fortunately, I have many people to thank, thus filling up this page nicely.

First I would like to thank Wendy, Deirdre, Sarah and everyone else in Mercier Press. It was an honour to be published by them and if the book is any good, it's because of their hard work.

To my family, who supported my ambitions of being a writer, I do apologise and can now prove that I was doing something when not tidying my room. Thank you Ceilinn, Cillian, Síofra, Fionn, Cian, Dad and Aunt Rose.

I would also like to thank Nellie for her advice, Gráinne for inspiring the title, and my various early readers: Rachel, Barry, Meredith and Síofra. Most of all, I would like to thank Laura Jane Cassidy, who read a very early draft and whose enthusiastic thumbs up and excellent advice are the reasons this book exists in your hands now.

Finally thank you, reader. I hope you liked it.

June 2018